Bred by the MINOTAUR

LYONNE RILEY

introduction

Hank has always regretted the last time he saw "Rapunzel," the woman who carried his first calf. He never asked for her real name, and he's thought about her nonstop ever since. Then, six years later, he gets his wish for a do-over when he goes in to breed her a second time.

Phoebe likes her job as a surrogate. Ever since she got too attached to her first client, she's learned to distance herself from her work—that is, until she's reunited with him. When Hank tells her about their son, Milo, and breaks confidentiality to give her his name, Phoebe is tempted to look him up. But she has too many responsibilities, and it risks too much heartache, to get involved with Hank's family.

When a freak fire puts Hank and Phoebe on a real-life collision course, can she really keep her distance from the single firefighter and their son?

CONTENT WARNINGS

May contain spoilers.

- Graphic depictions of sex
- Anonymous breeding
- Surrogacy
- Size difference
- Pregnancy
- House fire
- Firefighting and rescue scenes (with a child in danger)
- Hospital scenes
- Bondage play
- Use of a gag
- Vomiting
- On-page broken leg
- Threat of death
- Birth
- Lactation kink
- Alcohol consumption

PHOEBE

My hands are trembling, which I think means my nerves are getting the better of me. But who wouldn't be nervous? After weeks of preparation, I'm now strapped down to the breeding bench with my legs wide open, ready and waiting for whoever might walk in the door to put their cock in me.

I was supposed to use the dilator more, but it was such a strange thing to do, trying to stretch myself open. They told me in the paperwork to use it for two weeks, but I only did it for one because I've been busy at work, and my sister hasn't been doing all that well.

Still, I got the thing good and wide, and it's hard for me to imagine what kind of monster might have a dick bigger than that.

The long hand on the clock hits the hour mark, and on cue, the door behind me opens. I hear a *clomp clomp!* as my guest enters.

Hooves? What kind of creature has hooves?

Fuck. Maybe this whole thing was a mistake. Maybe

signing up to carry a monster's baby was an incredibly foolish decision. What if I can't go through with it? What if I freak out? We have to have *sex*. Sex, with a complete stranger!

Oh, and then there's the whole pregnancy part. If this works—which some hoofed creature in this room with me has paid good money for—I'll be carrying his offspring for a good part of the next year, depending on the species.

"Gestation time varies," the intake doctor at DreamTogether had said. So who knows how long the pregnancy could last? I can't discount the pain of birth, either. I've never done it before, and I only have other people's horror stories to inform me.

Hooves. Right. He could be a satyr, I suppose. Or a centaur. How would it work with a centaur?

"Hello," a deep voice booms, and the door closes. I go shock still, like prey playing dead. Maybe if I don't move, he won't notice me.

"Hi." My voice comes out weak and small. He can see all of me right now, from my ass to my clit. As he approaches me from behind, I wish I could cover myself. Instead, I'm out on full display, my legs spread so he has easy access to me. If he wanted, he could simply lube himself up and—

A large hand chastely touches my thigh. He strokes gently, like he's letting me know he's there.

"Are you nervous?" that deep voice asks.

"Ha," I manage. "Me? No. I-I'm not nervous. At all."

There's a snort, which I feel against my back in a small gust. "Don't worry. I am, too."

This piques my interest, but I try not to turn my head to look at him. This is supposed to be anonymous. We're not allowed to exchange any names or details, or we risk being terminated from the program completely. Though I don't think it's against the rules to know what species he is.

"But this is all for you," I point out. "You wanted a baby and arranged this appointment."

"That's why I'm nervous." That hand continues stroking my thigh comfortingly. "I've wanted this for so long, I don't want to screw it up."

Now it's my turn to laugh. "How could you possibly screw it up? All you have to do is put your cock in there and let loose."

There's a sharp intake of breath behind me, and soon there's another hand on my opposite thigh.

"'All I have to do'?" my visitor repeats. His palm ventures up and over the swell of my butt in a soothing motion. I think it's supposed to be soothing, but instead, it sends a shiver of electricity up my back. "Hmm."

He doesn't say more as he squeezes ever so slightly. Then his other hand moves toward the inside of my thigh, down to my exposed sex. I still don't know who or what he is, but he can't be human in shape with hands and fingers that size.

His touch is so close to my pussy that I pulse with anticipation, wondering when he's going to cross the distance. I tighten my hold on the grips to calm my racing heart as he simply traces the outside of me, wandering along the tender flesh of my inner thigh.

"It's not all I'll do," my visitor says at last. His finger slides over one of my lower lips, running along it down toward my clit. He pauses there, just shy of touching it, and huffs another heavy breath. I wonder when he's going to pick up the bottle of lube they left on the side table and get on with it already.

Not that I'm too eager or anything. But, fuck, maybe this guy's slow, easy tenderness is turning me on. Everything cranks up to ten when the soft pad of his finger glances over my clit, and my whole body shudders against the breeding bench.

The monster circles back to do it again, earning the same response. Languidly, he drags his finger down through the folds of my pussy, where I'm surprised to find I'm wet. All this teasing is winding me up, I guess.

He thoroughly soaks the pad of his finger there before returning to my clit. Now it glides easily, back and forth, and I gasp and jerk with each pass.

Soon, his other hand is slipping down between the cheeks of my ass like a heat-seeking missile. Once more, he teases me before going in for the kill, stroking my labia and spreading them apart. I can feel his breath against my pussy. Is he staring at me down there?

"Have you ever had sex with a minotaur before?" he asks after many long moments of silence.

I jerk out of my reverie. "No?" Though I suppose I know what he is now. A minotaur. Interesting. What does he look like? Is he one of those big, shaggy minotaurs, or a sleek black-and-white one?

He grunts, letting me know he heard me. I wonder if he's always this quiet, or if he really is just as nervous as he said he was. And of course, now I'm wondering what's different about his cock versus a human cock. I've never had sex with a monster of any kind before.

While he continues playing with my clit, which is making me wetter and, surprisingly, hungrier, his wandering fingers press into my pussy. I think he's going to put a finger inside me, but instead he explores, like he's studying the shape and size of me down there.

Then, he slips one finger in, and my body arches off the bench.

"Oh!" The sound tumbles out of my mouth. With his other hand still taunting my clit, that finger is exactly what I need.

"Do you like that?" he asks, slipping his finger in deeper and then pulling it back out.

I nod vigorously. "S-sure."

He pumps it a few more times before I sense a second one nudging its way in. He's playing me with both hands now, stroking two thick fingers inside me while gently rubbing my clit.

"Y-you don't need to do this," I manage. "It's okay if you don't want to."

He pauses. "Well, I want to."

Before I can reply, he pushes his fingers deeper, then curls them and strokes the inside of me. Oh, fuck, that's perfect. There's an erotic squelch as he fucks me faster with his hand.

"Ah, good." That deep voice reverberates up my spine. "You have a wonderful pussy."

Whoa. I tighten up at the compliment, and I hear him inhale sharply behind me. His circles on my clit speed up, and then, abruptly, they stop.

"Sorry," he says quickly, and I hear the snap of the bottle of lube opening. "I really need to be inside you."

I smile to myself, pleased that I've turned him on, too. There's another wet noise as he slicks the lube all over himself, and then hooves clomp on the floor. He grasps my ass, and I feel something... blunt and large and wet pressing at my entrance.

"Oh, wow. You're small." He sounds less aroused and more concerned.

"Don't worry. I used the stretching thing."

I can hear the smile in his voice. "'The stretching thing'?"

"It made my, uh, vagina wider. For you."

"For me." His voice travels through me again, going straight to my nipples. That wet object pushes harder, and then it slips through.

Oh, wow. *Wow*, is that bigger than I expected. My body strains because he's even broader than the dilator.

The minotaur presses in a fraction deeper. "Is that okay?"

I can barely speak because every neuron in my brain is firing on all cylinders. "Y-y-yes, that's... that's okay." Fuck. That's more than okay.

"Good." Then he slides in farther, more of that thick, wet cock asking me to open for it. On and on it goes until—

"Ow!" I bite my lip as he goes too far, and he bumps into something supremely sensitive.

"Fuck. I'm so sorry." He pulls back out, leaving me completely, and I whine at the sudden loss.

"Wait, wait, it's all right." I want him back. I need that glorious stretch. "Try again, just not as deep."

"If you're sure—"

"Yes!" I tilt my hips up, spreading myself even more open for him. I hear a rumbling, bovine low. When he grabs me, he grabs me harder, clenching my flesh with his fingers as he slides inside me again.

Oh, that's good. My earlier pain utterly forgotten, I roll back into him.

"Damn," he whispers to himself. "You feel so good. So tight and—" He reels his hips back, then shoves his cock into me again, "—so wet for me."

I nod rapidly, moaning as he maintains that even pace, only reaching in partway. He's so thick inside me that I can't even clench, can't even flex, and my body feels as if it might split apart at the seams.

And then, a finger brushes over my clit.

I gasp and my muscles tense, and my minotaur moans in return.

"So that's how I make you come." He lets out a thoughtful sound, and his finger picks up speed as he ventures just a hair deeper.

"There!" I cry out. That's where I need him. The strange head of his cock is rubbing over a wonderful spot, something that sends sparks of pleasure up into my throat.

He pauses, then withdraws slightly and pushes in again, repeating the motion. My voice comes out garbled, and I grip the breeding bench even tighter, bewildered that some stranger could pinpoint how to turn me into mush so easily. It's like he can read my body as he repeats this over and over, applying a steady pressure, until my moans have become helpless cries.

I've never been fucked like this before, and the worst part?

I'm never going to see this guy again.

two

HANK

THE WAY MY SURROGATE'S WATERFALL OF BLONDE HAIR cascades across her back, sliding to and fro with every thrust of my hips, is like the most beautiful artwork. I'm mesmerized by her, by the bouncing of her perfect ass, the sweet clenching of her pussy, the escalating volume of her moans.

Rapunzel. That's what I decided to call her as soon as I saw the straw-colored hair that looks like it would be marvelously soft under my fingertips. I don't dare touch it—that seems personal. But then I look down at my cock buried nearly halfway inside her and wonder why touching her hair would be too far over the line.

You only live once. I bury my fingers in those yellow locks as I slide into her again. Her head tips back, and I wish I could see her face as she moans.

Rapunzel. I hope I get to visit her again. I hope this isn't the last time I get to sample this incredible woman, because next time, I want to get even deeper. I want to train her sweet body to take me, and then fuck her like this many, many more times.

Ah, damn, this isn't good.

I've scrimped and saved for years just to have a child of my own, which isn't an easy feat on a firefighter's salary. Now I'm going to make sure I breed a calf into this lovely human, and what a baby we'll make.

But before I do that, I'm going to make her scream. It hadn't been in my plan, but now that I'm here, I want to make her come apart before I stuff her full. That's the least I owe her for doing this for me—for signing up for DreamTogether and making my wish for a family possible.

I target that place inside her that makes her cry out and try my best to thrust only to that depth, ignoring the way my cock is aching to go deeper, to fuck her faster, to come all over her and cover her in my smell. Closing my eyes, I focus on the sound of Rapunzel's escalating cries, the movement of my hand on her clit, trying to ignore the way my balls tighten and ache with my need to release inside her.

She's so tight now, impossibly tight, and I shiver, grinding my molars together as I try not to let off. I just need to maintain my methodical attack, and—

Rapunzel's scream echoes around the room. Her body clamps down around me, and the overwhelming pleasure of finally letting go nearly bowls me over. I slam into her, sheathing myself as far as I safely can, and my eyes roll back in my head as I shoot everything out. I pump again, trying to get it as deep inside her as possible, hoping it makes it where I need it to go. As much as I would love to do this again, every visit is an additional cost, and there's only so much I can afford.

I nearly collapse on top of her, my haunches shivering underneath me with the force of my climax. I look down at where my cock is buried inside her, and white cum dribbles out from her pussy, which is spread wide around me.

"Holy fuck," Rapunzel mutters, shivering. "I almost blacked out."

I wonder if that's a good thing or not. I don't want to part from her, so I stay that way, propping myself up on the sides of the bench. I'm hypersensitive now, but my cock is also still alert, to my surprise.

It wants to fill her again.

"Are you ready?" I ask over her shoulder, sweeping up her blonde hair into my hand and then running my fingers through it. She lets out a mewl as I move inside her, staying deep but rocking back and forth.

"For... for what?"

"For me to put a calf in you." There's a wonderfully obscene sound as I pull back, sending my cum sloshing out of her, then thrust in again. She moans pitifully, and her pussy responds in kind, flexing around me.

Good. Very good.

"Yes!" Rapunzel cries out as I set a languid, easy pace, warming her up again for me. "Put one in me, please!"

That's all the encouragement I need.

I fuck her again, grabbing her ass this time, and I don't even need to touch her clit to make her scream and fall apart.

I think I've found the perfect woman for me. I wonder if there's some way to find out who she is. Maybe I could take her on a date. Get to know her better.

But all that's against the rules. DreamTogether is very clear about the anonymity factor, and I risk losing everything by crossing that boundary between us. Still, as my cum spurts out of her, dripping down onto the floor as I pant over her, her screams still hanging in the room—I think that I'll regret not knowing who she is.

I wish I had a choice.

When the speaker comes on to tell us we're finished, I finally withdraw, my cock spent, and reach for the towel to clean her up. Rapunzel trembles, and she is good and red from where I took her. It is a beautiful sight, still wide from where I was inside her, dripping from how I stuffed her.

What is Rapunzel like? What does she do outside these walls? I am curious about all these things as I clean myself off, too, then put my boxers and pants back on.

"Thank you," she says weakly. I pause with my hand on the button of my jeans, my tail flicking as I listen. "You didn't have to... do all that."

"Oh, I did." I stroke her ass as lovingly as I can. "I very much did. I hope that... it all goes well."

Her head droops. "I hope so, too. Well, it was good to meet you."

"You, too." With one last pat, I depart the room, wondering what just happened to me.

I can't stop thinking about Rapunzel afterward. My thoughts have been riveted to her ever since I left that room, and they don't stop barreling onward even as I reach my empty house.

I live in a majority human city because it's easiest access to the fire station. Most firefighters are monsters, simply because we have the size, stamina, and helpful additional features to make us more effective. I work alongside a gargoyle who has stone skin during the day, and he can break down a flaming door without getting a burn.

Handy.

I look through the dark window into my house and shake my head. I bought this place nearly six years ago, when I was in my mid-twenties and thought I'd be settling down soon with a wife and family. That had been my hope, anyway—but a few years in, and still no sign of her.

That's when I started saving for DreamTogether.

I push open the door and flip on the lights. It's easy to imagine this house filled with excitement, laughter, my partner waiting to kiss me when I come home, and my children grabbing onto my legs. Now that possibility is at hand, minus the partner. It will be me and my future child. Mom and Dad have happily signed on to help out, and Mom is thrilled at the prospect of getting to babysit her future grandchild while I'm away at work.

My schedule is so all over the place that dating just doesn't work for me. And maybe I'm choosy, but it's hard for me to... well, get it up. Generally.

Today, on the other hand, was new. Rapunzel spoke to me in a way no one ever has. It was as if I could smell that she was right for me, and I hope today isn't the last time I see her.

I wait and wait for a call from DreamTogether. My surrogate will be taking a pregnancy test daily, checking to see if my sperm has taken. If it doesn't work within three weeks, they'll set up an appointment for just before her next ovulation.

Fourteen days after my visit with Rapunzel, my phone

rings. I'm at work on the bench press, and I set down the bar with Ron's help as I run for my phone.

"What are you so excited about?" Ron calls after me. I've been jumping up at even a spam call, wondering if I'll get to see her again, or if my new baby is on the way.

It's DreamTogether. I smash the answer button and hold the phone up to my ear.

"Hello?"

"Hello! This is Dr. Hodgens, and I'm calling because we have some positive results here from your surrogate."

I should be far more elated than I am at this news. Instead, all I can think is that I won't get to see Rapunzel again.

"Congratulations!" the doctor says on the other end. "Now, pregnancies are touch and go in the beginning, so don't get too excited until we're three months in..."

I stop listening because I already know what he's going to say. I'll get updates here and there from the doctor, who will relay information from my anonymous surrogate. Now the ball is rolling, and someday soon, I'll finally have what I've always wanted. A child of my own.

But something aches inside me, too, because I might have found the woman for me—only to lose her the moment I found her.

After that, I count the months.

One. Two. Three.

I get another phone call saying that the pregnancy is going well, and I'm left with a mixed bag of feelings.

Rapunzel haunts my dreams. I hear her cries, feel her

pulse around me, and wake up panting and sweating at the memory of her.

Where is she? What is she doing? I wish I knew. Sometimes in the middle of the night, I make crazy plans, trying to figure out how I could get in touch with her.

But then I would sacrifice everything.

Eight. Nine. Ten.

The time draws nearer, and I'm a bundle of nerves. How is Rapunzel faring with our calf inside her? What kind of father will I be? It feels like I haven't truly slept since I first went into that room and bred her.

It's right at the start of the eleventh month that I get the call.

"Your surrogate has gone into labor," the doctor tells me. "Get prepared for our call to come pick him up."

Him. I'm going to have a son. Finally, after all the money and all the waiting, I'm going to be a dad.

I wait on the edge of my seat for the next call because the room upstairs for the calf has been ready for months. I hope that Rapunzel is all right, that the birth isn't too difficult for her. I wish I could be there, holding her hand, watching as our infant comes into the world.

I stay up all night waiting, and it's only when I'm starting to doze off in the morning that my phone rings.

"Your son is waiting for you."

He's perfect. Milo is perfect. He looks just like me, as the doctor predicted—the monster genetics always win out. But he has bright, almost neon-blue eyes that shine out from his speckled white and brown face. I can only see them when he stops crying, but they are beautiful.

Hers. That is the piece of Rapunzel I'll always have.

three

FIVE YEARS LATER...

PHOEBE

Here I am again, strapped in and ready to rumble. My legs are held open by the stirrups, my pussy exposed and waiting for whoever walks in that door. The breeding bench underneath me is padded, and the frame is solid steel to tolerate whatever my visitor today has to throw at it.

I'll be prepared for whoever it is. My client could be a demon, or a cyclops, or maybe even a gryphon—doesn't matter to me. I have a job, and I'm good at it now.

It's a simple gig, really. Take a monster's cock. Get pregnant. Carry that pregnancy to term. Hand over the baby. Mostly passive, though it is physically taxing. I've made it a habit to keep up with my exercise, and I'm lucky my body is naturally good at recovering.

So far, both of my pregnancies have been different in terms of symptoms, though neither too difficult. I've heard horror stories from the other surrogates about carrying a monster's baby, both during and after, and I'm glad that hasn't been me. Not yet, anyway. Cross your fingers and toes, knock on wood, et cetera.

That's why my ass is up in the air, my legs and hands strapped down so I stay safe even as a monster goes wild. It's time for baby number three.

The door behind me opens with a creak. Though I know the point of DreamTogether is anonymity, I can't help being curious about who it'll be this time. I wonder what it would be like to see their face, to know who's inside me, who's shooting in all that sperm that will eventually become a living thing.

"Hello," I say when my visitor doesn't speak at first. I hear a *clomp, clomp* as hooves pass over the tile floor. Perhaps a centaur. Or maybe another minotaur. That would be an odd coincidence.

Fuck, that cock. After that, I was sure that I'd break confidentiality just so I could learn who he was. I felt in my bones that something was different about him, and what we'd done wasn't just procreating. We had connected on another level, something deeper than just bodies doing what they were made to do.

I knew him, more than it makes sense to know someone you've never even seen.

But I didn't obey my impulse. I need this job, what with my sister's medical bills stacking up, and I couldn't risk it by breaching confidentiality. That's grounds for immediate termination—and they would withhold the rest of my payments, which I certainly can't afford.

We didn't see each other again, and I think my heart broke a little the day I found out I was pregnant. It broke more every day until the baby was born, and I handed it off without even knowing what it looked like.

Let's just say I learned some important lessons. Never get too close to a client, no matter how good they fuck you. It's just a job, and feelings only make it harder.

It was difficult to give up that baby. When I watched them carry it away, it made me ask all sorts of uncomfortable questions of myself. What if I could have kept it? Could I be a mother?

What if I wanted to be a mother to that child, and now that chance was gone forever?

The day I came home from the hospital, I sat on my bed curled in a ball, wishing I could have seen the father's face, maybe held his hand. After that, I pledged that I'd never let myself get swept away by one of my clients again. And I held fast to this agreement with myself during my second pregnancy, doing my best not to get attached to the baby growing in my belly.

That one was easier to hand off after the birth, but I still wonder what that child is doing now, where they are, what their life is like.

I've been waiting for my visitor to answer my greeting, but still, he doesn't even speak to me, and I get a creepy-crawly feeling down my back. Is he going to stay silent like this as he does the deed? I guess that's fine, but even some friendly courtesy would be appreciated, especially if we have to meet a few times for this. If he's going to put his cock inside me so I can carry his baby for the next who-knows-how-many months, the least he could do is say "hello."

"Okay then," I say in a clipped tone, because he clearly doesn't want to reveal himself. "Get to business, why don't you?"

Then, a huge, soft hand brushes over the swell of my ass.

"You look exactly the same," comes a quiet voice, as that hand smooths down my skin. I shudder all over as it skims the crease between my ass cheeks to the other side.

Wait. I know that voice, that delicate hand.

It's *him*.

HANK

I wasn't quite honest with my mother about where I was going when I asked her to babysit Milo for the afternoon. I didn't tell her I had an appointment at DreamTogether, though I can't exactly say why I kept it secret.

Maybe I was afraid she wouldn't approve of me bringing home a second baby when Milo is already so much to handle. He's almost five now, and he's always moving at the speed of light. I'm planning to get a nanny this time around, but Mom will surely still be involved.

Maybe I was afraid she'd judge me for using my inheritance from my father this way. His passing a few years ago was hard on all of us, but he left me enough that I could do this.

Hell, maybe Mom wouldn't have judged me at all. No, maybe I didn't tell her because I didn't want to admit why I'm going back now.

On the surface, it's because I want a sibling for Milo. But it's also very much for Rapunzel.

Here she is again, spread open for me on the breeding bench, her legs strapped in to hold them apart. I can see everything, from her tiny, puckered ass down to the flower between her legs, its petals leading to a pronounced clitoris. I would know that pussy anywhere.

I caress one of those familiar soft cheeks. Already my cock has recognized her, too, and it extrudes from my sheath inside my jeans.

"It's you?" Rapunzel asks, her voice catching. "Really?"

I nod even though she can't see me. "It's me."

Her blonde hair is cut short now, in a bob around her head that shows off the slender shape of her neck. Rapunzel doesn't really fit her anymore, but that's all right. I'll learn her real name soon enough, I hope.

Last time I was here, I was much sloppier with her. I won't be sloppy this time. How often have I thought about her since then, jacked off to the memory of her small body swallowing me up, the sound of her little mewls and moans? She'd taken me so well—*so* well—and I regretted everything about the last time I left this tiny room.

If only I'd known it was our last chance, I wouldn't have gone without finding out her name, her email address, her phone number.

Well, now I have another shot.

"I never thought I'd see you again," Rapunzel says, gasping when I squeeze her ass. I'm watching with interest as that small slit between her legs pulses. "Well, 'see,' relatively speaking."

"I thought the same." I test her other cheek with my other hand, squeezing it as well to see if it has the same effect. Her pussy opens and then closes again with her breaths. "But here I am."

"Here you are," she echoes. I bring my thumbs down to trace the outline of her soft folds. Each of her pinkish labia swells as I tease her.

"Are you ready?" I don't even touch her there. No, I

simply run the pad of my index finger down to the hood that hides everything but the tip of her clit. "Are you ready for me to put another calf in you?"

At these words, her pussy flutters again, and the pink inside is already starting to glisten with moisture.

"I can't believe it," she says instead of answering, and her head turns to one side like she's trying to get a look at me. "You're back. After..."

She swallows, and I don't speak as she turns forward again.

"Sorry," she amends quickly, straightening. "None of my business."

Is she supposed to pretend we've never had a calf together before?

"I requested you," I tell her, spreading my fingers on one hand to run them along the ridges of her pussy, from the bud to the tiny slit. I can't believe that I fit in there.

"Oh," is all she says as I rub up and down again. Her hips lift into my hand, urging me to stop teasing and dive into her, but I deny her body's request. "Why me again?"

"I want my son to have a sibling." Now that Milo is out of his baby years, I want to fill up the house with even more laughter, and ensure Milo has someone else in his life to play with—someone who will always be there for him, and who he can always support and love.

"A son..." she says, trailing off. "That makes s-sense." Her voice breaks when I slide one finger down, between those plush lower lips, to the treasure underneath. "A brother or sister."

"Indeed."

"DreamTogether was..." She gasps as I press that finger into her, testing how wet she is for me. "...fine with that?"

"They're fine with money." And I'm not the only one

who's ever requested the same surrogate twice. It's common practice among repeat clients.

A giggle makes Rapunzel clench up around the pad of my finger. I squish it deeper, toward that tiny slit that I'll eventually open wide around my cock. Just as she pushes back, drawing me in, I drag my wet hand away and down to her hood, then brush over the tip of her clit.

Rapunzel jerks, and now her pussy is weeping for me, leaking down over my fingers. I swirl it all up and glance over her most sensitive spot again, this time with more pressure, and she moans.

I remember just what to do with her.

Returning to her small entrance, I take my time pushing the pads of my fingers inside her.

She whimpers underneath me. "I can't believe—" I withdraw, then slide back in again. "—you're back."

"I'm back," I croon, leaning forward so I can brush my haunches against her legs. "That's where my cock will fit." I squeeze my hand in deeper, then curl my fingers to stroke her inside. Her hips snap up, and so I stroke again, and again, falling into a steady rhythm. Then I reach down with my thumb and brush it over her clit.

"Oh, fuck," she gasps, her body tensing. "That's... that's so good."

"I remember what you like," I tell her, leaning farther forward so now my hand is pressed against my own crotch as I fuck her with it.

She nods rapidly, clearly in agreement.

Good. I studied in my dreams.

When she's nice and wet for me, I take a third finger and soak it in her juices before attempting to slide it in. Again her ass bucks into me, and I groan as it forces pressure back against my cock under my jeans.

I don't know how long I can do this. But I need her to open for me, otherwise I might not be able to do what I came here to do. Well, one of the things. I remember how small she was before, and I'm going to make sure we fit together easily this time.

She squirms as I work my finger inside her, and it looks like she's prepared well for me. Good. I pump all three of them, stroking the spongy inside of her as her cute little moans escalate. I fuck her with my hand until she's dripping into my palm, and then hastily I withdraw it, nearly tearing my jeans in my rush to get them open. Once they're on the floor with my boxers, I stroke myself, earning a white bead at the tip of my cock. My balls already feel tight as I imagine what she'll feel like.

Rapunzel tries to turn her head again. "Please," she whimpers at the absence of my hand. "Put it inside me."

My tail thrashes at the eagerness in her voice. I step up to the bench, then press the blunt head of my cock against those spread, swollen lips. Taking a deep breath, I push in.

Her cry is unrestrained, and there's no feeling in the world like being inside her again.

four

PHOEBE

Oh, he feels even better than before.

Since my first time at DreamTogether, I've learned to use the dilator for two weeks as suggested, and I made sure to be prepared for today. So when the flared edge of the minotaur's cock works its way into me, I'm ready for its size—but not at all for how wonderful, how thick and heavy and yet *giving* it is inside me.

He huffs against the back of my head. "You feel incredible," he groans, stopping himself before he goes too deep. He learned.

Then he pulls back, gripping my ass with one hand. When he shoves himself in again, it lights up every last one of my nerve endings like a Christmas tree. "I missed you."

I wonder if he intended to say those words as he pumps again, pushing deeper, asking for even more of me to open for him. I collapse forward against the bench, gripping the padding under my hands tightly as he rocks into me, sliding in farther before pulling out.

Saying *I missed you, too* doesn't quite encompass how I feel about hearing his voice again. For the nearly eleven months I carried his baby, I thought of him. Fantasized about him. Eleven months I grew it inside me, wondering where he was, what he was doing, what he would think. When I went into the delivery room with my sister holding my hand, I had wished it was him there with me, making sure the baby came out safely.

Today, he confirmed for me that I have a son out there. I was always aware of it in the back of my mind; I carried it, after all. But after the baby was taken away and returned to their father, I tried never to think about them. That wasn't a good path to go down.

But now the minotaur is back. For me.

"I'm glad you're here," is finally what I say. I'm glad it's *him*, that I could have him one more time.

His exploration of my body slows. Remaining sheathed in me, he leans down, trailing his hands over my bare hips, up under my shirt. A wide nose whiffs at my hair, and then those hands slide loosely back down to my ass.

"Did you know," he says quietly, right behind my ear, "that he likes broccoli?"

He pushes his cock into me slowly, tantalizingly slow.

Does he mean... our kid?

"Our calf's name is Milo," he whispers, plunging into me again, pressing that blunt head deeper. I gasp and fall forward as he fills me, stopping just before he would bottom out.

We still hadn't worked up to his full length last time. Maybe this time will be different.

"Milo," I repeat, keeping the words tight against me so the overlords at DreamTogether can't overhear us. "That's —" I moan as he speeds up his thrusts, remaining at the same depth that's sending shockwaves all across my central nervous system. "—a wonderful name."

And it is. Adorable, perfect.

"I always hoped you'd like it," he murmurs, settling deep inside me. There he rocks his hips, just sampling me, testing me. "I've thought about you a lot as he grows up. Wondering what parts of him are me, and what parts... are you."

I cry out as he pushes into me again, and then even more of him fills me up, stretching me, demanding that I widen and lengthen. I wish I could reach out and touch him.

As if he can read my mind, a hand drifts up my back, down my shoulder, to my knuckles. There, I look down to find his massive fingers wrapped around the back of my hand as he crouches over me. They're brown splotched with white.

"He's so rambunctious," he says, just for me, "getting into all sorts of trouble, like calves do." He's so calm, so quiet as he thrusts in and out, his hooves dragging on the tile as he pumps into me. I'm flying higher and higher, and somehow his words are twisting up my emotions into pure pleasure.

We have a child. His name is Milo. He's *rambunctious*.

I wonder what he looks like. What are his other favorite foods?

As my minotaur wraps his body around mine, he slams in, burying an obscene amount of that seemingly endless length inside me so I cry out. Each thrust is stimulating everything, his furry balls brushing over my clit each time he pounds into me—I'm vibrating, tense all over with my desperate need to orgasm.

"Come for me," he murmurs, and I do. I do, completely, utterly, my whole body clamping down tight around him and the bench and everything, and I don't even realize I'm screaming until I hear the echo of my voice around the room. The minotaur grunts against my neck and jams himself in one more time.

Then he roars. It's a powerful, rumbling sound, and immediately I feel his hot seed surge inside me, so much that it's spilling in a torrent down my legs. His roar morphs into a bovine low as he pumps again, releasing even more.

"Hank," he whispers in my ear as he remains lodged inside me, his heartbeat thrumming in time with mine. "My name is Hank Pittsfield."

HANK

I need her to know who I am. I need her to... what? To want to find me? To seek me out, beyond this room, and meet our calf?

Yes. That's what I want. Now I'm going to put the ball in her court.

Slowly I pull out of her, and my cock falls thick and wet between my legs. Her sweet pussy is gaping, spilling over with my seed. I wonder if I'll have to visit a few times.

That would help me convince her.

I rise to my full height, dragging my fingertips down her back so she shudders. Rapunzel is spent, lying limp on the bench, and I'm gratified I could please her so well.

Someday I'll train that pussy to take all of me.

I cup my hand under her and catch my spend as it dribbles out, then I use two fingers to spoon it back into her, her battered pussy squeezing around me again. She moans, wriggling against my hand, and already my blood is flowing south again.

A speaker crackles. "You're almost out of time," a voice says, as if they know I was about to fuck her yet again.

I sigh and reach for the towel to clean up both of us, being gentle with her reddened sex. She took so much of me, I'm proud of her.

Then I tuck myself back into my jeans, and slowly my cock retreats into its furred sheath. All I want is to walk around this table and look into her eyes, to finally see her face, but I don't want to push her. Not yet.

I position myself behind her again, as if I'm about to take her a second time, and lean forward so I'm speaking behind her ear.

"Thank you," I whisper.

She turns her head slightly. "Hank," she repeats quietly, so the mics can't pick us up. "I'm... I'm Phoebe."

I nod gratefully, then pull away. "I'll see you again soon."

"I hope so," she answers.

Me, too.

When I get home and step in the front door, I'm immediately tackled by a moving ball of fur and stubby horns. Milo wraps his arms tight around my legs, squeezing me for all I'm worth.

"Dad!" He disengages, peering up at me through his shaggy hair. I really need to cut it soon. "Where did you go?"

"I told you," I say, stooping down to scratch behind his ear. "I went shopping."

"Oh, right! Did you buy anything for me?"

I shake my head. "No, sorry. But I'll find the right thing to get for you soon."

He doesn't need to know yet about the breeding bench. I'll cross that bridge when I introduce them.

When. It's an *if*, really, whether or not she'll take my offer. I should be easy enough to find now that she has my full name, thanks to the internet.

Phoebe. What a lovely sound it makes.

My mother is in the kitchen, cleaning up the lunch she made for herself and Milo.

"Leftovers are in the oven. Just turn it on for ten minutes." She closes the dishwasher and dries her hands. "How did it go?"

Milo has already sprinted off into the other room to find Darla, our cat. They're connected at the hip.

"Like I said, I just went shopping. No big deal."

"Hmm." She sniffs the air. "Do you have a secret girl-friend, Hank?"

I blanch. "What? No. You'd be the first to know if I did."

She surveys me with narrowed eyes. I hate how moms can do that—see right into your soul. It sure helps when I haven't gotten a chance to take a shower yet.

"Then who did you just have sex with?"

I fist a hand in my hair and stumble back against the counter. "Ugh, gross. None of your business."

"If it's not a girlfriend," she begins as she starts the wash cycle going, "then did you go back to DreamTogether?"

I should have known it was foolish even to try to hide it. My shoulders sag.

"Yes. I did."

Mom turns to face me, her arms crossing. "Why didn't you just tell me that?"

I fumble for the right words. "I didn't know what you'd think. I just... I had to do it, and I didn't want anyone to try to stop me."

She tilts her head. "Why would I stop you?"

I hate when she forces things out of me like this, just asking innocent questions. It's a tactic that works every time.

"Because I know Milo is a lot, and I'm not married, so I'm doing this by myself, which means *you* have to step in and pick up the slack all the time. But I'm going to hire a nanny for them this time around, so—"

"I don't have to do anything," my mother says with infinite patience in her tone. "I like spending time with my grandson. Just like I'll enjoy spending time with my other future grandchild."

I huff and glare down at the floor. She's really trying hard to make me feel guilty about lying to her now.

"Did you see her again?" Mom asks, more gently this time.

My head shoots up at the question, and a little smile crosses her face.

"Thought so," she says. "Milo's mother."

"How did you know?"

"I remember what you were like back then," she says, reaching into a cupboard to pull out a tin of shortbread cookies. I'm surprised when she opens it and there isn't a sewing kit inside, but actual cookies. "After your first visit with her."

Was I that obvious? I try to think back to it, but all I can remember from that time is Rapunzel. *No, Phoebe.* My hormones went wild after mating with her, and I had to jerk off twice, sometimes three times a day for a few weeks just so I wasn't hard all the time. It's rather awkward when you spend twelve hours per shift with three other people, trying to be normal.

"Afterward," Mom clarifies. "I remember *afterward.*"

"Oh." Now I understand. When I got the call that my surrogate was pregnant, and I wouldn't need to visit again…

I hadn't been in the best place, that's true. But I thought I put on a better face. I didn't know Mom even sensed anything was wrong. The understanding that I'd succeeded in impregnating Rapunzel but not seeing her, not smelling her, not burying myself in her while she carried my calf? That had sent me sinking like a lead weight.

"Why didn't you say anything?" I finally ask, snatching one of the cookies out of the tin and breaking it between my wide teeth. "If you knew all this."

Mom reaches out and brushes a crumb off my chin, even though I'm not five, like Milo. "I didn't think it would help. You wanted to suffer alone. I thought it would pass, but then it never did. Even when Milo came, you weren't the same."

I go to wipe my hands on my pant leg, but she holds out a napkin I didn't realize she had. I grunt as I take it, then lean back against the counter.

Thinking back on it, maybe she's right, and I haven't really been myself since the last time I walked away from Phoebe. Not until today.

"I gave her my name," I finally admit. "I put it all out there."

Even though it's risky with all my funds invested in DreamTogether, I had to do it. Phoebe is special—I know it.

A pleased, warm smile crosses my mother's face. "Good. I'm sure that if she feels the same connection you do, you'll hear from her." She pats my shoulder. "And I'm excited for a new baby. Don't get a nanny."

Then she leaves the kitchen and starts tidying up Milo's scattered toys. I don't know how I got so lucky as to have her for my mother.

It's almost time for my shift, so I go looking for my little bull calf. He's up in his room, gently petting Darla on the head while she soaks up the attention. Ever since he was little and I told him to "be gentle" with her, he's always petted the cat like this, just gently running the palm of his furry hand over her head. She purrs, tilting her face so his hand is rubbing over her cheek instead.

"Darla told me today that she doesn't actually like eating mice all that much," Milo says when I sit down next to him on the bed.

I raise my brows. "Oh? But she sure likes to catch them and drag them in through the cat door."

"Yeah, but she just does it because mice are bad. She thinks they taste gross."

Hmm. It does rather sound like something a cat would say.

"I have to go to work, buddy," I tell him, scratching between his knobby horns. They've been growing in slowly but surely, though they won't start to really take off until he's in his teens, when the hormones hit like a tornado. "I'll be here in the morning, though."

He frowns. "We haven't gotten to play *Monster Masher* at all lately."

"I know. I'm sorry. But Larry's taking one of my shifts next week, so we can play *Monster Masher* all day if you want. All right?"

Easily swayed by promises, Milo grins up at me. "Okay, Daddy."

Fuck. It still hits me right in the gut when he calls me that. I reach down and pull him against me, wrapping him up in my arms as tight as I can. I will protect him from everything in this entire world.

Milo squeaks, then laughs and returns my hug, not realizing there are tears in the corners of my eyes.

Phoebe. I can't wait for you to meet him.

five

PHOEBE

Hank Pittsfield.

It would be so incredibly easy to get online and look him up. I'm sure there are dozens of people in the world named *Hank Pittsfield*, potentially quite a few minotaurs, but I'm certain that I'd know him if I saw him.

I don't think he's the type to smile much. No, he's strong and sturdy and quiet, but commanding and dirty when he needs to be.

I wonder how old he is, and where he lives. What does Milo look like?

I feel like a limp noodle my whole drive home. Hank really fucked me into a puddle.

Hank. I wonder what it would be like to have sex with someone like that all the time. What if we had sex face-to-face? I've never done it outside DreamTogether with a monster, certainly not a minotaur.

Does he have a wet nose, like a dog? What would it be like to fuck someone covered in fur? *Or is it hair on minotaurs?*

This is what happens when you live mostly celibate. My sex life hasn't been fabulous since I took this job, but it's not like I have much spare emotional energy for dating or hookups.

The moment I think it, my phone rings in the passenger seat. I pick it up with the car phone.

"Feebs," my sister says, "is today garbage day?"

I glance at the clock on the dashboard screen. "It's Monday, garbage day is Tuesday."

"Okay. That's good. We didn't miss it."

My sister... is a worrier. When she first got sick, we weren't sure whether it was nerves or illness. Now she has plenty of things to worry about, in addition to all the other things she was already worrying about before.

"I'll take it out when I stop by later," I tell her.

"Oooh! You have to dish everything about your appointment today. I want to know who the next baby daddy is."

I assure her I will and hang up the phone. That's the reason I don't date, for the most part. When I'm not with Sandra, I'm working at my desk over my tablet, designing a beauty ad. Not much time in between, especially when you're pregnant a third of the time. I haven't tried pregnancy sex yet, but I'm not that interested.

When I get to Sandra's place, I find the gnomes that sit out front have been rearranged again by the neighbor kids. When she feels well enough to get up and move around, she'll move them back to where they were before—or maybe she'll set them up in a parade this time.

Inside, everything is exactly where it should be, and my indoor slippers have been moved from the careless place I left them last time and back to the rack by the front door. Sandra's on the couch, knitting needles in hand, when I come inside.

She attempts to jump off the couch, but she's not quite strong enough and she has to sit back down immediately.

"I tried," she says, turning off the television and setting her current project aside. I can't tell if it's a scarf, a sweater, or a blanket. "Now come on, tell me. Who was it this time?"

"The minotaur." I'm still woozy from our session, and as I sit down, I don't feel like I've quite returned to my own body yet. "*The* minotaur."

Sandra squints. "Wait, the first guy? Baby daddy numero uno?"

I nod, because I don't have words for how confused I feel right now.

"Wow. He came back for a second go? He wants a whole other kid?" She leans forward to peek into my face because I'm still staring down at the floor. "You look bamboozled."

"I think I'm bamboozled," I answer, pushing some hair away from my face and sighing. "That was not what I expected today. At all."

"You were sad about that guy for a long time." Sandra puts an arm around my shoulders. "What was it like seeing him again? Or... whatever it is. Having his dick in you."

I snort-laugh. "It was amazing." I knew I'd never forget him the first time around, but after what he did to me today? "Incredible. Like, life-altering. And he said all this... stuff."

I choke for a moment, thinking about what Hank whispered in my ear.

Sandra leans in. "Like what?"

"Like, about our, um... the first one. You know."

Her eyes get huge. "Wait. He told you about the kid?"

"His name's Milo," I say, my voice already starting to shake. "H-he likes broccoli. What little kid likes broccoli?"

"A minotaur kid?"

"He said..." My voice shakes. "He said Milo is rambunctious. A-and... the minotaur, h-he... he gave me his name."

Sandra's been stroking my back this whole time, but now stops.

"His real name?" she asks. "Isn't that against the Dream-Together rules?"

I nod rapidly. "Very much so. He could lose his entire deposit and get banned from the program for good."

"He wants you to find him," Sandra says right away. "Obviously. He wants you to look him up on social media, or in the phone book, and call him."

"I know." It was obvious. Why else would he have given it to me if he didn't want me to find him?

Sandra gives me a mystified look. "So? Why aren't you on the computer right now?"

Now it's my turn to peer at her like she's turned into an alien. "Why? Because DreamTogether is anonymous. That's the whole point!"

I don't realize I've raised my voice until Sandra cringes.

"Sorry," I say more quietly. "It's just... if I did it, if I broke anonymity, I could get kicked out of the program forever, too."

"So you're not going to look him up?" She cocks her head like a curious bird. "Why? You obviously dig him."

"I don't know anything about him." I make sure to keep my voice down even as I start to get riled up. "He's a stranger. That's why both of us did the program. He pays me to have his kid, and then he gets the kid back, and we never see each other again."

"But—" Sandra begins.

"I can't lose this job," I say suddenly, taking her hands in mine so she can really understand. "I can't. If DreamTogether found out, what then?" I gesture around us at my sister's quaint house. "We don't get to have this, Sandra, if I lose this job."

She studies me, and it's baffling to me that she's not nearly as upset as I am.

"Is that really what you're worried about? Because if he's the one who broke confidentiality, he's probably not going to tattle on you to DreamTogether. What if he just wants to ask you on a date?"

"That would be even worse! I can't date the guy while trying to have his baby. Especially not a guy with a kid."

"*Your* kid," Sandra points out, and I just want to strangle her.

"That's the cherry on top," I snap. "This isn't some adorable meet-cute from a movie. That's a real kid's life. What if we go on a date, and he wants me to meet Milo? I'm his biological mom. And this entire time, we're lying to DreamTogether?" My breath is coming fast just thinking about it.

Sandra gently clasps my shoulder. "Hey, Feebs. Breathe for a moment. None of that has happened yet." She pulls me in close. "Come on. Let's just check the guy out. Maybe you'll see his picture and be turned off right away, and it won't even be a problem."

She slips her laptop off the coffee table and pops it open, heading to her social media, where she types in the name: "Hank Pittsfield."

There are tons of results, as I expected. She filters them by state, then city. All the results vanish except two.

It's obvious which one is *my* Hank Pittsfield. One of them is a human man in sunglasses, taking a selfie in a car. The other is... well, a minotaur.

A very jacked, very enormous minotaur. A minotaur that

could lift a car. A minotaur that could probably throw me around like I was a child's toy.

Thinking about *that* minotaur's cock inside me today, my body is instantly electrified.

"Holy shit," murmurs Sandra as we click on his picture to expand it. Both of us lean closer to the computer.

Hank is brown and white in a big splotchy pattern, with short-cropped hair that is adorably striped in the same manner as his fur. He has two rounded white horns that curl up and forward. In his profile picture, he's shirtless and wearing orange pants, and he looks like he's posing for something.

"Is he a fucking *model*?" Sandra says, lurching back from the screen. She points at it, and then at me. "You are going on a date with this guy. You are sending him a message, right now, and inviting him to get Italian food."

I can only gape at the picture.

This is worse than what I imagined. So, so much worse. It would be astonishingly easy to fall in love with someone like that, who's absolutely cut, who has the serious face I expected, who whispers dirty things in my ear along with sweet, loving things, and wraps his hand around mine on the breeding bench while he talks about our son.

"I can't." I shut the computer closed and stand up. Sandra gives me a startled look. "No. There's a reason they do it this way. So there are no complications. And this promises to be very complicated."

"But Feebs—" Sandra starts.

"I said 'no.'" I head into the kitchen, hoping this will be the end of the conversation. There's dinner to cook, then I have to go home to get some work done before bed. I've got a tight deadline to meet, and my appointment at DreamTogether has set me back some.

"That's not fair," calls my sister. "You can just leave the room and I can't follow you!"

I don't answer as I busy around making grilled cheese sandwiches.

Looking down this road... I can't do it again. Once already I wished I could have something more with Hank—and then I never saw him again.

I can't risk that heartbreak a second time.

No, Hank Pittsfield is not something I need in my life. I have enough on my plate as it is, and going on a date with a gorgeous minotaur who has a son at home is not on the menu. Even if I were to entertain the idea, it's too risky with DreamTogether.

When I return with two sandwiches and set one in front of Sandra, she doesn't speak. Instead, she turns on the television again and we eat in silence while watching *House Swap*. After I've taken the plates to the sink and put them in the dishwasher, I find Sandra waiting with her hands crossed on her lap.

"Phoebe," she says, and I stop in my tracks at the use of my full name. "You're an adult woman, and you deserve to have happiness. I'm thinking that maybe I should get a nurse to come over and—"

"We can't afford that," I interject.

"Maybe I move out of here," Sandra says. "What if I came to live with you so we didn't have to pay for this place anymore? Then you wouldn't have to deal with DreamTogether, and you could do what you want."

I'm stunned into silence.

She's right that we'd save a lot of money that way. But I also know we don't do well when we live together. We went through years of it as teenagers, and we were always at each other's throats. It's not healthy for us.

"I don't want anything to change," I say at length. "I like it the way it is now. I don't need a boyfriend, especially one who has a kid."

My kid, my brain adds.

"All right," Sandra says with a sigh. "I won't push." Her expression is sad, though. "But I hope you'll keep your heart open, Feebs."

I turn to her and put my arms around her. "My heart has everything it needs."

She just hugs me back, not saying a word.

six

HANK

I DON'T HEAR FROM PHOEBE AFTER OUR SESSION AT DreamTogether. I check my phone regularly to see if she's finally found me and sent me a message, or perhaps a friend request, but there's no sign of her.

Did I make a mistake? She must not have felt what I did, that deeper connection between us.

What did I expect? It's just sex. Literally. We've never seen one another face-to-face. The pull I feel is merely hormones and chemicals, driving me to mate with her over and over and—

Damn it. All I want is to hold her in my arms, to fill her up with calf and then keep her close to me while she grows it. To be there to hold her hand, to see our new one get big and strong, to give her every food she likes and rub her back when she's sore.

Fuck. Will she tell them I tried to break our anonymity?

After a week, my hope for hearing from Phoebe turns into dread. I've already paid for the full DreamTogether package. If I'm found out, I'll lose it all—the rest of my inheritance.

But I get no call from them, either. She must not have told on me. Yet.

My mother tries to comfort me when two weeks go by, and there's no word.

"If it's meant to be, then it will be," she says, but it does nothing to make me feel better about the mistake I've made.

Soon though, it's time for Milo to start kindergarten. We go school shopping for new clothes and some supplies. As he stands in front of the mirror in his snappy outfit and new backpack, my eyes sting. I'm always amazed at how fast he grows, from one stage to the next before I can blink.

When we go in for his first day, I lead him by the hand to his new classroom.

"I can't wait to meet my teacher," he says, skipping along beside me as he jumps over cracks in the pavement. "I want to do lots of coloring."

For only being five, Milo's very passionate about his art. I hope he keeps his love for it as he grows up. Maybe he'll be a fantastic artist someday.

"I think your teacher is excited to meet you, too," I say as we walk through the halls. His new teacher, a goblin named Mr. Felk, is waiting outside the classroom door. He introduces himself to Milo, and Milo forgets all about me as he rushes into the class to meet his classmates. I wave and call goodbye, but he's already absorbed in making a new friend.

I leave feeling deflated, wondering how long it will be until Milo doesn't need me to walk him to class anymore.

When I make it into the station, my coworker Ron arches an eyebrow at me.

"You look even more miserable than usual," he says,

pouring a mug of coffee and handing it to me, his huge wings stretching and then settling behind him.

"Milo's first day at kindergarten," I say, taking a big gulp even though it burns going down. "Hard to see them not need you anymore."

"Wait until they're teenagers and they know better than you about everything, and all they want from you is chauffeuring."

"So much to look forward to," I say morosely, sitting down at the communal table and grabbing a bagel.

"Aren't you trying for another one?" Ron sits down next to me. "You really want to do all that baby stuff again?"

That's exactly what I'm looking for. I miss the days when Milo cried for my attention and asked me to sleep in his bed so the shadow living in the closet wouldn't get him.

"Yeah," I say. "I do."

Ron shakes his head. "Why don't you ever date, man? There are tons of eligible women who would drool over Milo."

There's only one woman I want, though. But she's not interested.

Life returns to normal—as normal as it can be with a wound in my chest. Mom doesn't bother me anymore about Dream-Together, knowing it's a sore spot.

Still, I hear nothing from Phoebe. One night I even try to look her up online, but there are far too many possible matches, and I don't even know what she looks like besides a bob of blonde hair.

Then I get the call confirming my next breeding appointment. Good—at least it didn't take the first time, so I can see her again. I hope she hasn't withdrawn from the program after my invasion of privacy. What would I do if I walked in that room and found someone else there waiting for me?

I would leave. I don't want anyone else to be the mother of my calf but her.

As I sit in the waiting room, I clench my hands into fists to channel my anxiety. When they call me up, all my nerves are in overdrive, anticipating what I'm going to find on the other side of that door.

When it opens and I step inside... there's a familiar woman strapped to the breeding bench, her legs spread and her wonderful pussy exposed to me. Her ass is a perfect pale pink, and when I close the door behind me, she flinches.

I don't say anything as I approach. I'm already getting hard for her, seeing her like this again, but it feels tainted by the weeks of silence in between.

"Hi," she says quietly when I skate one hand over her butt.

"Hello." I sigh as I pull my pants down, and my cock leaps out, ready and willing to serve. It's never been like this with anyone—even at home watching porn, I don't find it this easy to get hard.

I don't speak further as I reach for her clit and gently stroke it. Her hips jerk, and she lets out a little gasp. I continue methodically, rubbing her until her pussy starts to gleam, and her lips are swollen and pink. She wriggles under me as I slip one finger inside her, then two, pumping them in time with my beating heart, but she never says a word.

I've fucked it all up, and I'm too much of a coward to say anything, either.

When I feel certain that she's ready for me, I pump some

lube into my palm and cover myself with it. Even though it's cold and the room feels small, my body is ready to slide into hers again.

I push the head of my cock into those swollen lips, and she moans as it slips through. Then I'm finally inside her again, where my cock and my heart both feel I belong.

Her moans morph into cries as I thrust deeper with each stroke, and I can't help but relish the feel of her around me, so warm and wet, so delicious and inviting. Her beautiful ass shakes with every thrust.

I need her. I need her so badly that all the stiff walls I've built around myself crumble like dust. I want her in my life so much, I'll do anything.

So I lean forward, placing my hands over hers.

"Milo started school," I whisper in her ear. She stiffens under me, only to go limp again when I sink deep into her. I remain there for a moment, simply rocking back and forth. "He was so excited. He got a new backpack with kittens on it, and no one has said anything about a boy taking a kitten backpack to school."

I duck my nose under her hair, lipping at the back of her neck, and she tightens powerfully around my cock.

"Today," I murmur to her, sliding my hands up and down her arms until they erupt in goosebumps, "I'm going to pump you full. And you know what will happen next?"

Her channel flutters around me as she finally says, "What?"

"Then I'll put another calf in you." I thrust even further in, then yank myself out and tease her with just the tip. "It'll grow so well in your belly."

She squeezes around me even more, so I keep talking. I'm not much of a talker, but for some reason, with Phoebe, I can't stop—even as she remains quiet.

"It'll be such a wonderful calf." I thrust a few times experimentally, to see what gets the biggest reaction. She twitches and moans when I angle up, so I do it again, and again, as her sweet noises grow in volume. "And when it comes into the world, it will be so loved."

Phoebe cries out as I almost fully sheathe myself in her small pussy, and my eyes roll back in my head at the sheer, catastrophic bliss of being with her again. My balls are tightening, my spine rippling with pleasure. I stand up, holding onto her hips to get better leverage.

Then I really fuck her.

"More," she whines. "Please, more."

So I give it to her. I bury myself up to the thick fur at the base of my cock, and my balls slap her clit. She cries out, so I reel back and do it again, aiming up for that spot inside that gives her joy. She's clamping down tighter and tighter, drawing me in even more, squeezing all around me.

Fuck, I need this woman. I need to have her.

She's mine.

PHOEBE

Why does that guy have to be so absolutely phenomenal at this?

There's nothing in the world like his fat, heavy bull cock sliding in and out of me, whisked along by how unbelievably wet I am. As my body clenches, I can feel even more of him, that blunt head dragging across my sensitive lining. I feel like I'm above my body, watching Hank fucking me, every meaty last inch of him. Now, after seeing his photo, it's easy to imagine his big head with the long muzzle, teeth gritted as he pounds into me with his strong hips. I wonder if all the muscles in his abdomen contract with each movement. I can feel the fur of his thighs against mine when he leans forward again and traces his hands up my spine, then ducks under my shirt where my breasts are pressed into the padded bench. There, he meets my bra, but he pinches through it to get to my nipples.

I try. I try to play it cool, to not let him know how hard it was for me not to reach out to him. This is a job, I told myself. Anonymity is important. I need this.

But then I fall apart.

"Oh, fuck," I cry out as Hank picks up the speed of his frantic thrusting. I'm drowning in him, completely owned by him, used by him. "Ha—" I stop myself just in time from saying his name. But he hears me anyway, and starts thrusting even harder, even faster, slamming into me, sliding me around on the bench so the straps bite into my flesh. He fists my breast roughly through my shirt.

"And these," he whispers to me, nibbling the shell of my ear. "They'll get so heavy, so full."

Hank groans behind me as my body clenches. I'm so close, and with every new dirty thing he says, I get closer. I'm hurtling through space, the straps digging into my ankles and hands keeping me rooted to the earth. He stands back up and grabs my ass, digging his fingers into my flesh.

"There we are," he says as my orgasm weaves up my throat, through my hands. I'm screaming now as he ravages my body like I'm a limp doll. "Come all over my cock. Suck me dry."

Then, the world explodes. Hank is grunting, "Yes, yes," while I convulse, completely overtaken by my bliss. He keeps going, drawing it out further, sending fresh new echoes through me. I can't control the sounds coming out of my mouth, and then he growls, "I hope you're ready for all of it."

When he comes, he thickens up so full inside me that I clench the grips on the bench as tight as I can, holding on for dear life as he spurts, one warm jet after another, the pump of his hips punctuated by his moans. He slowly comes to a stop, still encased fully in me, both of us breathing hard in rhythm. I'm pulsing around him, and he's twitching in return.

"Maybe we have time for one more," he hums, experimentally reeling his cock back just to slowly push it in again, causing cum to gush down my thighs and onto the bench. I'm already so electrified that I arch into him, and we start a second time.

seven

HANK

I'VE NEVER HAD A HIGH LIKE FUCKING PHOEBE.

When I finally pull out of her, her lovely pussy is red and dripping with me. I rub the cheeks of her rounded butt and lean down to lick her. I want to taste all of her, especially while covered in me. Our scents mixed together is enough to drive me wild.

Then the speaker crackles. "Time is up."

I have to go now. But I still have one last chance to convince her.

I lean down again. "No one has to know," I say into her ear, keeping my voice very low. "Not DreamTogether. Not even Milo." She stiffens under me as I nuzzle the back of her neck. "I won't tell a soul."

Then, her breath comes out in one *whoosh*.

"I can't," she murmurs, so quiet I almost can't hear her. "I can't. I can't fall in love with you, Hank."

What?

I'm utterly baffled by this response. I open my mouth to

answer when the door behind me opens, and the attendant says, "Your session is over, if you don't mind."

I hurriedly clean us off, then put on my jeans, all while we're watched. There's nothing else I can say to her now.

I can't fall in love with you, Hank.

I'm puzzling over this as I buckle my belt, then hustle out without saying goodbye.

I stand next to my car for far too long, one hand on the door.

What did she mean by that? Is she trying to say that she's... in a relationship?

Of course, that's what it was. Damn it, I feel like a fucking idiot.

She didn't try to contact me before because she's already seeing someone. Maybe she's even *married*, and I just didn't get the message. No, because I'm a jackass.

I should never have told her about Milo and put that on her. I should never have come back here, to DreamTogether, at all. In fact, if I weren't such a monumental dipshit, I would have realized a long time ago that there was nothing between me and Rapunzel except the breeding bench.

I hope I haven't disrupted her life too much already with my antics, with my misplaced hope that she would want something more from me. But she's at DreamTogether for a reason, the same as I am. She's a professional at this. She doesn't want personal complications.

It's like flirting with your masseuse. I'm disgusted with myself.

I bump the roof of my car with my fist and get in. I took the day off so I could pick up Milo from school and spend the afternoon with him. When I made those plans, I thought I would be in a much better mood after seeing Phoebe again today.

But my anger at myself fades when I park at the school and go into Milo's classroom, where I find him happily scribbling on paper with a marker, surrounded by other kids playing and screeching as they get their backpacks to go home. He looks up when I walk in, and his face turns radiant.

"Dad!"

I pick him up and hug him, then I set him down and we walk out holding hands. We have a big day planned, and I'm going to put all of my heart into it.

PHOEBE

I told him the truth. I can't be what he's looking for, and I'm not available in the way he's hoping.

Back at home, I try to get some work done, but it's impossible to keep my focus on my task. My mind flits back to Hank, remembering how expertly he knew what to do with me, how to treat me, how to make me scream. Eventually it's time to head to my sister's to make dinner and help her out around the house until I drag myself home and go to bed.

I'm a little sore between the legs when I get in my car. I took all of Hank today—and I feel absolutely euphoric. If I hadn't had to tell him the truth at the end, I would have rather liked to fly away together.

But that's not an option for me. For *us*. For so, so many reasons.

My sister gives me the side-eye when I arrive, but this time, she chooses not to ask me about my visit. She's probably hoping I'll spill it on my own, but I don't want to admit that I shut Hank down. She'll be disappointed, what with the way she's imagining this playing out like some rom-com movie.

Dinner passes quietly, until suddenly, Sandra slaps the table.

"Come on," she says. "Tell me *something*, Feebs. I'm dying. What did you say to him? I mean, you basically didn't call back."

"I shut him down."

And we had the most unbelievable sex of my life. Again.

But sex does not a relationship make. Hank's just confused by all the signals his brain is sending to him. I know because I'm feeling it, too.

"Wow, that's rough," Sandra says. "How'd he take it?"

"I don't know. We were... interrupted."

She arches a brow at me. "What about next time? Won't that be awkward?"

"We don't know if there *will* be a next time." Just the thought of it, though, sends a shockwave of regret through me. I hope that's not the last time I see Hank, but there's a very real chance it will be.

I have to stop thinking like this. It would be for the best if it worked this time. Then I can move on with my life, get through the next eleven months, and then I won't have to think about him ever again.

A few days later, I take my first pregnancy test. Negative.

Though I breathe a sigh of relief, maybe it would be better if I didn't see Hank again, not after how I shut him down. I don't know that I can face him, metaphorically speaking.

A few days after that, I take another one, and watch as the line changes color—a single, bright pink line. If it doesn't come up positive in the first few weeks, the chance is very slim that we succeeded.

Then, as I watch, the second line forms. I stand in silence as it appears in the window and starts to turn bright pink, too.

Positive.

A big breath whooshes out of me. The disappointment is so big and sudden that I have to lean on the counter.

But it's for the best. This is what he wanted—another child. I'm going to make sure he gets it, even if I can't give him anything else.

All test results need to be verified in the lab, so I make a call to DreamTogether and they bring me in for an exam the next day. I can barely get through my work, tapping my stylus on my tablet until just the sound of it is driving me crazy.

If they verify this result, that's it.

I drum my fingers on the steering wheel the whole drive to the clinic. First I pee in a cup, and then I'm brought into an exam room. The middle-aged woman who greets me has me strip down and dress in a gown so she can verify the result with an image.

"There we are," she says, gesturing to the screen. I don't see anything. "We've got a stem growing. We'll bring you in for a follow-up appointment in a few weeks just to make sure the early pregnancy is proceeding as expected."

I nod numbly as she departs the room, letting me get

dressed again. I walk through it robotically, now that everything is all wrapped up in a neat little package.

I'm pregnant. Again. With Hank's child. His sperm found its way inside me and merged with my egg, and now it's taken root. We did what we set out to do.

So why does it feel like the world is ending?

It's late in the afternoon, so I go by Sandra's house first to cook her an early dinner. I need to go home and be alone for a while tonight, maybe work on my latest personal project.

I told my sister I went to the clinic this afternoon, and my face must give away what happened there.

"So you're pregnant again, huh?" she asks as I start cooking the macaroni. "Baby number three."

There's a five-pregnancy limit, and I don't know what I'll do after that.

"Yup." That's all I say. "No more Hank Pittsfield."

"No more Hank Pittsfield," she echoes.

We're both quiet all through dinner, Sandra occasionally trying to make conversation, but my mind is too far away.

Finally, I drive back home, and my head feels like it's full of water. Things will go back to the way they were before now. I don't need to think about Hank, or about Milo, and all the complicated things that come with them. I can return to my regularly scheduled life.

When I get home, I dump my purse and head to my tablet where I usually sit and work late at night. After my day job, I switch over to *my* work. Right now, I'm painting koi fish in a pond, trying to get the reflections on the water just right.

But I feel nothing looking at it. I have no urge to paint, so instead, I shed my clothes and head for the bathroom. I light the candles around the tub as it fills, then drop in a bath bomb for good measure. Once the bath is filled, I slide into the warm water and let out an immense sigh.

He likes broccoli.

My son, who's out there in the world somewhere, likes broccoli. He's rambunctious and has a kitten backpack. I wonder what he looks like—how much of me he has in him.

Hank said he wouldn't tell anyone if I contacted him. If we met in the real world, he promised it didn't need to be complicated, and we wouldn't get discovered by DreamTogether. But it would inevitably become complicated, given the fact we already have one kid and there's another on the way.

Complication is the last thing I need in my life. I don't want a boyfriend, a family, when my plate is already full. And someone like Hank... He can't break my heart again if I don't let him inside it.

I lie back in the tub, drifting lower and lower as the warm water seeps into my skin, heating me from the inside out.

I'm never going to see him again. I'm never going to touch him with my own pair of hands. It's over now, and we have no more reason to interact.

I don't realize I'm crying until a tear slips over my lips, tasting salty. I simply close my eyes and let them fall, sliding down in the water until just my face is above the surface. I can't help but wonder what it would be like if I did reach out to him, if I did send him that message, if we did meet face-to-face.

Would we have sex again? How would it feel to look in his eyes as he took me?

Slowly, everything fades into darkness. Except for that photo of Hank in the orange pants, the sound of his low voice in my ear, his warm hand skimming up and down my back. His marvelous cock, slowly rocking inside me, bringing me higher and higher until I'm a hot-air balloon ready to pop.

I'm carrying his child again. What will he say when he finds out?

I'll never know. My mind breaks free of my body, floating up above it, letting me drift away to a place where I can forget about all of this.

REE! REE! REE!

I snap awake at the shrill shriek of an alarm. And when I open my eyes...

Everything is on fire.

eight

HANK

WHEN MY PHONE RANG AND I SAW THE CALLER ID, I KNEW. IT
was DreamTogether, ringing to tell me that I've succeeded,
and my surrogate is pregnant.

There's no more need for me to come in again and
see her.

I'm out of chances. Now I'll never know who she is. I'll
never meet her. I'll never get to find out what she looks like,
what kinds of foods she enjoys, how her face looks when
she's being pleasured. I'll never get to lick her small pussy
with the prominent clitoris, the soft petals of it swollen and
waiting for my cock. I'll never get to feel her around me
again.

I stare down at the phone blankly as the person on the
other end asks, "Are you there, Mr. Pittsfield?"

"I'm here," I manage. "Thank you for letting me know."

Then I hang up. Milo's playing with Darla in the other
room, building a little house of blocks around where she's

been sleeping on the floor, but when I look down I find him standing next to me.

"Dad?" he asks, tilting his head. "Who was it?"

I open my mouth to answer, then close it again. I haven't rehearsed yet what to tell him because my mind has been too preoccupied with Phoebe.

"It was the baby factory," I tell him, coming up with something on the fly.

"Baby factory?" His eyes grow huge. "What did they want?"

"They're letting me know another baby is on the way to us." I rub his head, scattering his shaggy hair. "A little brother or sister for you."

"What?!" His mouth is round. "Another baby? For us?" He thinks through this for a long moment, then gives me a huge smile. "I can't wait for them to meet Darla. And Grandma, too. Grandma will like that."

I can't help but smile. "I think she will, too."

Milo skips back into the other room, making little *beep boop* sounds. "A sister or brother!" he crows so loudly that Darla gets to her feet and hurries out of the little fort he's built with blocks. "Did you hear that, Darla? A baby!"

I'm so glad, monumentally glad, that he's excited. This could have gone much worse.

When Mom stops by later, I give her the good news. But I can't seem to summon much excitement for it, because of what it means.

She rubs my back. "I'm sorry she never tried to contact you."

I shake my head, slipping into a chair at the dining room table. "No. It's totally understandable why she wouldn't. What if she has a boyfriend? What if she has other kids of her own? I don't know anything about her. I shouldn't have told her anything. I shouldn't have—"

"Coulda, shoulda, woulda," Mom says. "You did what your heart wanted. And this time it didn't work out, but following your heart is never a bad thing."

I want to believe that's true, but it will be a long time before my heart isn't sore anymore.

Once Milo's settled in with his grandmother, I head off to work. News has spread with my coworkers that I was trying again for another kid at DreamTogether, and they all slap my back when I tell them about the call today.

"The world's most eligible single dad, blowing his entire wad on having another kid," Ron says disapprovingly. "Surely it can't be that hard for a guy like you to get a girl."

There's only one girl I want, and if I can't have her... there's no point, really. Milo brings me all the joy and love and satisfaction I need in life. And so will this new baby.

Eliza's brought in donuts tonight, so we're all sitting down to eat one when the alarm goes off. As we're programmed to do, we jump to our feet and head for the truck, Ron calling out orders. He hops in the driver's seat and I'm in the passenger, with the others in the back. The door to the garage reels open, and with the sirens blaring wildly, we drive off into the night.

"Five forty East Fourth Street," the dispatcher says, and Ron swings a quick right. Cars move aside for us as we blow past them.

"There," I say, pointing at the smoke billowing up into the sky. Another right and then a left, and the house comes into view, flames consuming the entire south side. When we pull up out front, everyone jumps out.

An older woman is shrieking as my coworkers unwind

the hose. "She's inside! She's inside! There's a lady living there!"

Fuck. Without thinking twice, my training kicks in, and I head straight for the house, throwing my mask on as I run. This is where my size comes in handy.

I smash my shoulder into the door, splintering it. Then I rush inside, searching for a hallway that would lead to a bedroom. Likely she was in her room sleeping, so that's the first place I look. The smoke clogs the hall, making it hard to see.

Then I hear someone yelling behind a closed door. She probably tried to get out, but the handle was too hot.

"Get back as far as you can!" I shout. Inhaling a big breath, I smash into the door just like I did the previous one, blowing it into pieces.

Inside is a bathroom, and the fire is licking the wall of the shower. In the corner by the toilet huddles a small, naked woman with short blonde hair, her eyes huge and her hand covering her mouth to keep out the smoke.

Without a second thought, I kneel and grab her, and she struggles for a moment before I say, "I'm saving you. Hold on tight."

Then I turn around and run back the way I came, protecting her from the flames with my body. My uniform has fire retardant, and the safest place for her is in my arms.

When we burst out into the night, she's coughing and gagging. I set her down on a lawn far from the flames, which my coworkers are already hosing down. The terrified neighbor kneels next to us.

"Phoebe?" she says to the blonde woman. "Are you all right?"

Phoebe?

It can't be.

"I'm…" The blonde coughs again. "I'm all right. I think." She gazes up at me, opening her mouth to say something, when she registers my face.

"Hank?"

The world around us comes to a complete stop. It really is her.

And damn it all, even with her wet hair in shambles and ash covering her face, she's gorgeous. With cropped blonde hair, a button nose, and pure blue eyes—surely she's the most beautiful creature I've ever seen.

PHOEBE

I barely register it's not just any minotaur standing in front of me, but Hank himself, before I'm consumed by another coughing fit. He pats my back, running his hand around in soothing circles.

"There are EMTs on the way," he says, crouched on his furry haunches in the grass. More sirens wail in the distance.

"My house," I whimper, taking in the sight of my home consumed in flames. I barely register that I'm completely naked, and the crying starts before I can stop it. "I can't believe it. My house. M-my…" I can't get the words out around my sobs as I curl up in the grass, trying to cover myself.

Two big arms wrap around me, pulling me in close to a warm chest.

"Yes, but you're alive and safe," Hank says. "That's what matters. You have homeowner's insurance?"

I nod as best I can, pressed tight against him.

"Then it'll be fine."

"B-but my photos, my computer, m-m-my *life*!" Everything I own is in that house. Everything I've ever treasured. My memories. My clothes. It's all gone.

Hank holds me tighter. "I'm sorry."

But this is my fault. I know it is. Those fucking candles.

I sob harder and Hank holds me, protecting my naked body from prying eyes until an ambulance pulls up. EMTs surround me, and Hank releases me as they haul me up onto a stretcher. I reach for him because he's my safety right now, the only thing I have left.

He turns back to the fire, then to me again as the EMTs wheel the stretcher into the back of the ambulance, a blanket tossed over me.

"Hank!" I call out, because I don't want him to leave me, not now. I don't want to be alone.

He approaches the back of the ambulance.

"I'm her boyfriend," he tells the EMT. Then he calls out over his shoulder to one of the other firefighters. "Ron, I have to go!"

"What?!" the big gargoyle calls back.

But Hank hops in anyway just before the ambulance doors close, and it drives off.

He takes a seat nearby while they put an oxygen mask over my face.

"Her vitals are okay," says one of the emergency responders. "She needs oxygen, and then we'll find out how much smoke she inhaled."

Again I reach for Hank, for a familiar face, and he takes my hand in his as the howling ambulance drives.

"It'll be okay," he says, squeezing my fingers tight. "You'll be all right."

But it's not me I'm worried about. It's everything. It's my whole life, gone up in a burst of smoke.

When we reach the hospital, I'm wheeled out again on the stretcher, dressed in a hospital gown, and brought into the emergency room. Hank stays close while doctors and nurses check my vitals again, keeping me on oxygen.

"No serious damage," the doctor says with a sigh of relief. She turns to Hank. "You got her out?"

He nods quickly.

"Happy coincidence that her boyfriend is a firefighter." She arches an eyebrow. "I'll leave you two alone. She should be fine after a few hours on oxygen. Her heart isn't working too hard and seems stable for now."

Then we're alone, the heart monitor beeping next to the hospital bed. Hank scoots his chair closer and takes my hand again, rubbing his thumb over my knuckles.

I shouldn't be thinking about it at a time like this, but damn, he's hot in his fireman outfit. It can barely hold in how big he is, and his thick, muscled body looks about to burst out of it.

"How did you know it was me?" Hank asks at last, still holding my hand. "You've never seen me."

I turn my head, realizing I'm found out.

"I did look you up," I say with a cringe. "I... I had to know."

Soft fingers cup my chin, and I open my eyes as Hank turns me back to face him. His expression is serious, but there's a startling gentleness in his face.

"I'm glad." He doesn't release me, his hand traveling up my cheek. "I'm so happy to finally see you."

For just that moment, I can forget. For just that moment, I'm absorbed in him. His big muzzle ducks down, toward my mouth, and then he hovers there, so close it would be infinitely easy to press our lips together. And I'm about to kiss him when I remember where we are—and why we're here.

Hank Pittsfield shouldn't be here, too.

I pull away abruptly, fully retreating onto the bed. Hank jerks back, his eyes wide with surprise.

"Oh, fuck, I'm sorry," he says, as the same realization crosses his face. "I'm so sorry, Phoebe. This isn't the time or the place."

But it's not that. It's how much I wanted it, how much I craved it, how much my heart was singing for it in the midst of all this chaos. It's how badly I want to throw myself at him, for him to kiss me and hold me while I cry on him, that makes me put a good distance between us.

"It's okay," I tell him with more sureness in my voice than I feel. "You saved my life tonight."

Hank bows his head. "Just doing my job."

"Lucky for me you were the one on duty." I offer him a small smile. "Shouldn't you go back to work, though? You didn't need to come all this way with me."

His only reaction is his cute little cow ears pressing back against his head. "Yes, I did. I needed to know that you were all right." Then his brow creases. "You told them about the calf, right?"

"Fuck," I mutter. Surely inhaling all that smoke won't be good for the baby. "Go get a nurse. It's probably fine, since you got to me before it got too bad, but we should make sure."

Hank quickly nods and hops up, running out the door with a *clop! clop!* of his hooves.

I fall back on the bed, ruing the day Hank came back to DreamTogether. Now he's not just a photo on a screen, or a cock and a pair of hands—he's a living, breathing minotaur, who just saved me from a burning building.

I squeeze my eyes closed. My house. My artwork. All those college photos saved on my computer. The letters we wrote our parents that got returned to us. So many things now gone forever.

All because of me.

PHOEBE

WHEN THE NURSES COME BACK, HANK QUIETLY SITS DOWN again.

"Are you the father?" one asks, and he nods. I'm wheeled into another room and he tags along. There, a new doctor performs an ultrasound just to be sure the fetus is all right. Hank is silent by my side the whole time, watching from the chair next to the bed. His presence is immeasurably reassuring as the doctor searches.

"It's stable," he says at last, and both of us breathe sighs of relief. "Everything looks good."

Finally, after hours upon hours in the ER, they've determined I'm well enough to leave. I should call Sandra, but I don't have anything, not even my purse. No driver's license, no money, no phone.

When it hits me, I start to cry all over again, thinking how much work it will be to repair everything I've lost. Birth certificate, gone. Social security card, gone. How will I pay my taxes?

"Hey, hey," Hank says softly, rubbing my shoulder but not sitting too close.

"Everything is gone. The deed to the house. The title for my car." I sob harder. "My records, my receipts..."

"Fires happen. There are procedures in place."

As comforting as Hank's voice is, the emptiness, the hollow spot where my life used to be, is an uncrossable void.

"I need to see my sister," I say finally, sitting upright. I don't even know if my car is still there or if it caught fire, too. "Could you... drive me to her place?"

I feel bad asking him for anything after turning away his kiss earlier, but Hank eagerly agrees.

"No problem. The station isn't far—I can go get my car."

"Don't you have to go back to work?" I ask for what feels like the millionth time. Hank firmly shakes his head.

"I'm going to get you where you're going safely. You're carrying my calf, for starters. And... I want to make sure you're all right."

He's so fucking sweet, it hurts.

"Don't make me cry again," I croak, wiping my face. That pulls a small smile out of him.

"Cry all you need. I'll go get the car if you stay here."

I nod, and Hank quickly hurries from the room. When he's gone, I lie back and stare at the ceiling, already beginning to make a list of everything I'll have to do to recover my life, beginning with a call to get new documents.

I have to remind the world that I exist, when all that's ever proven it before is some ink on paper.

HANK

I jog the ten or twelve blocks back to the station, and I don't even go in to check on the guys before grabbing my keys out of my locker and hopping into the car.

One more chance. I have one more chance to convince Phoebe to give me a shot.

Now I know she's not married, and she's probably not dating anyone, because the first person she asked to see was her sister. But she's also just lost everything, and I can't even imagine how that feels. I need to help her, to do whatever I can to ease the pain of what she's gone through and what's to come.

I can't be thinking about those big blue eyes and that small pink mouth this way.

Then I'm on the road to the hospital, where I park out front so I can bring out Phoebe. She's dressed in clothes that don't quite fit her—something the nurses must have provided from the lost and found—and she's sitting up in the hospital bed when I arrive. She smiles wanly as I enter the room.

"Hey, thanks." She gets up, and I'm about to offer her my hand when I think twice about it, settling for holding the door open.

When we get out to the car, Phoebe hops easily into the passenger seat, and I breathe a sigh of relief that she's all right after everything that happened tonight. I won't say it out loud, of course, but it could have been so, so much worse.

I try not to think about that as she tells me which direction to drive. Her scent fills up the whole car, and I have to work just to keep my eyes on the road.

She starts leading me toward my own neighborhood,

and I wonder where her sister lives. We're some of the few monsters in a mostly human neighborhood, so I suppose I shouldn't be surprised that we're close by.

When we turn into my housing development, though, I start to feel nervous. Is she going to think I'm stalking her when I tell her I live right around the corner?

We stop on the street just across the block from my own home, where the houses are smaller.

"This is going to sound nuts," I say as we stop. "But I live right over there." I point down the street at my own front door.

Phoebe's mouth drops open. "Really? Right there?" Her face falls, and I don't think she's pleased by this news. "Oh."

"Sorry," I say reflexively. "When I got hired at the station, it was easier and closer to live here."

She gives me a baffled look. "You can't help where you live. Anyway, thank you for the ride. And for..." She takes in a deep breath and closes her eyes, like she's steeling herself. "For saving my life." Her voice cracks, and she buckles forward in the seat.

Phoebe's not crying, not that I can tell, but it's like all the pain and hurt in her body is trying to force its way out. She shudders, and without thinking I wrap my arms around her, drawing her across the console.

"I'm sorry," I say quietly into her hair, stroking the back of her head. Phoebe doesn't pull away. No, her hands fist in my clothes as she shakes with even more force.

Then she peels herself away, and reluctantly, I let her go. She sits up straight in the seat and gives me a firm nod.

"Thanks again, Hank," she says, and climbs out of the car. I'm tempted to walk her to the door, but that would be ridiculous, so I simply watch as she heads up to her sister's house. There's a rather interesting arrangement of lawn gnomes in the well-kept, though tiny, yard. When the door opens and her sister appears, I drive away.

Around the block.

I can hear them reuniting, and a voice that's similar to Phoebe's but much higher and louder cries out. This must be her sister finding out about the fire. I should give them some privacy, so I park the car and head inside.

Finally, I call the station to let them know what happened.

"She's the mother," I explain to Ron over the phone. "I had to go with her and make sure she was all right."

"Wait, *what*?" I can almost see his big stone brows squinting. "From DreamTogether?"

"Yeah. She was the one in that house."

"And she's okay? The calf?"

"All fine." I let out a sigh. "But I'm exhausted."

"Go to bed, Hank," Ron says. "I'll wrap things up here with an incident report and get your sig tomorrow."

With that we hang up, and I stand in the dark kitchen, breathing through my nose.

"Honey?" Mom appears at the door, a mystified look on her face. "You're home early."

"Bad fire tonight." I want to say more, but it's too much to explain right now. "I need to sleep, but I'll tell you in the morning."

She gives me a concerned look, then heads back to the guest room.

When I get into bed, though, sleep is the last thing on my mind. No, what I'm thinking about is Phoebe, only a block and a half away. Phoebe, the most beautiful woman in the world, who's carrying my calf. Phoebe, who barely escaped a fire with her life.

I replay it over and over again, the moment she recognized me and relief filled her face. Now that I've seen her with my own two eyes, I don't know if I'm capable of letting her go again.

I roll over in bed, thinking of how I almost kissed her tonight, how she almost returned it before pulling away.

I can't fall in love with you, Hank.

What did she mean?

PHOEBE

"I can't believe it," Sandra says, hiccuping. "Everything was in there."

We cried together for a while on the couch when I told her about the house. Before I came over with the news, she was feeling stronger than usual, able to walk around and arrange the lawn gnomes. But now she's down and out for the count again.

I realized too late that Sandra's documents were in the house too, in a filing cabinet along with mine. Now we both have to pick up the pieces of our lives.

"At least those letters are gone," she says, shaking her head. It's always been a point of contention that I kept them.

After Sandra and I had been taken by the state as kids, we tried to write home to our parents, but all our letters were returned.

Not undelivered. *Returned.*

I've kept them to remind myself what kind of people our parents were, and how I would never become like them.

"Well, you can sleep on the couch," Sandra says, right as the sun starts coming up. "Let me get the pillows."

"It's fine. Go to bed. I'll handle it." I know where every-thing is, anyway. It's all labeled.

Sandra nods and heads to her bedroom while I make myself comfortable on the sofa. If I had my phone, I could find that photo of Hank. That's what I wish I had right now—the warm arms he put around me in the car. Maybe then I could sleep.

I wake up a few hours later to bright midday light coming in the windows, and I blink bleary eyes. Once Sandra's up, too, I'm able to log into my work email from her computer and tell my boss what's happened.

All my equipment, gone. Horror dawns on me as I realize every piece of art I've ever created, every design I've ever done, has now vanished along with my machine. All my backup drives were in the same place as my computer—inside the house.

I'm beginning to melt down when Sandra finds me. She's also exhausted from a lack of sleep.

"You had a cloud backup, right?" she asks tentatively.

"Just essentials. Work stuff was all backed up to the company shared drive, but nothing p-p-personal..." Tears leak from my eyes again, and I wonder if I'll cry for the rest of my life. "Nothing personal survived. It's all gone."

I think of the koi painting, only half finished but one of my best pieces yet, and burst into sobs.

Sandra makes me some cereal for breakfast because that's the most she can do on her feet, while I use her phone to call the bank and order new credit cards. It's all so tedious, so terribly trite, each call I have to make just to pay for food.

I still won't have a way to pay in the meantime, and I can't withdraw cash without a driver's license, so I'll just have to make do with what Sandra's got.

"You know everything that's mine is yours," my sister says, putting her arms around me. "We'll get through this, Feebs."

I try to feel her confidence, but it's so far out of my reach.

My work gives me a week off to get my life straightened out again, but I don't think that will be nearly enough time. At least my car was safe from the fire, since my garage is full of crap and I park it on the street.

I fall asleep in the early evening to the sound of Jeopardy, a half-eaten box of Chinese food sitting on the coffee table. My dreams are all filled with fire, swirling upward into the air, taking everything in the world that means anything to me along with it.

ten

HANK

Knowing Phoebe is right down the street makes me rock hard.

The mother of both of my calves, the woman I've been hungering for going on six years now, is only a few houses away.

I explain to my mother the next day how I happened to be sent to a fire—and it was my surrogate's house.

"And after all that, she still hasn't messaged you?" Mom says, tut-tutting.

"She doesn't even have a phone anymore." And probably no way of buying a new one. "Hey, where's that old phone we were talking about giving to Milo when he's older?"

Mom thinks for a moment, then heads into the other room to rifle through drawers. She returns with a beat-up old smartphone.

Since I have no way else to contact Phoebe, I decide to simply walk down the street and knock. I think this could help her, but I don't want to come across as clingy and worry her more.

Not if what I think is true—that she does, actually, quite like me. But that's what frightens her.

After a few moments, the door opens and it's Phoebe, dressed in clothes that don't seem to fit. She lets out an undignified noise when she sees me, then slaps a hand over her mouth.

"I'm still in my pajamas, sorry," she says, bunching up the baggy clothes in her hand. "I thought you were the postman. I asked for some stuff to be overnighted."

"Sorry to bother you." I hold out the phone quickly. "I know last night you didn't have anything. I thought you could use this until you get a new one."

She stares down at the phone, and then gingerly takes it from my hand. She's looking at it like it's a golden egg.

"Wow," she says, her eyes scrunching up as if she's trying to keep from crying. "This is really nice, thank you."

"Hey." I calmly reach out and squeeze her shoulder. "It's nothing. Whatever I can do to help, just tell me."

Her big blue watery eyes search mine, and then she sighs, closing them.

"I really appreciate it," she says.

I glance around the small house behind her, where pillows and blankets are piled up on the couch.

"Are you going to a hotel?" I ask. "Insurance should pay for one."

"I've been trying to get help all day, but filing a claim is going to take forever." She sighs and withdraws from the door. "I should probably get back to it, actually." She clutches the phone to her chest. "And thank you for this. It's a real help right now."

I nod. "Of course. Let me know what happens."

"I will."

"If you find you need a place to stay..." I shouldn't be offering this, because I know she'll turn me down—but I also want her to know it's an option. "I have a spare bedroom. For the..." I nod downward at her. "For the calf."

She blinks, then glances down at her own belly before turning her eyes back to me again.

"You could move in there. I know that I'm, well, a stranger, but..." I trail off, realizing I've already said too much.

Phoebe's mouth works like she isn't sure what to say next. "That's a really kind offer, thank you. But I think I'll be all right on the couch."

I know right away that I've overstepped. In my humiliation, I say a hasty goodbye, then hurry back off down the street as the door closes behind me.

Man, I made an ass of myself.

I stalk back to my driveway, irritated at how I really am like a bull in a china shop. I just don't know the right things to say. All I know how to be is honest, and I wish I could convince her to trust me, just a little. I want to help hold her up while the world is falling down.

PHOEBE

I mean, I barely know the guy. So why did I want to say "yes" so badly? Why did moving into Hank's spare room sound like the best idea anyone's ever had?

All I've got here at Sandra's are some misfitting clothes

and a couch with sinking cushions. He would have a whole room, a bed, just for me.

There's no way I could do something like that. He's right—he is a stranger. We don't know each other at all, not beyond a few anonymous encounters at DreamTogether.

I file my claim with insurance, and I'm told that at some point, my house will be rebuilt, exactly the way it was before. Whenever they get around to it, though.

"It could take two years," the woman on the other end tells me.

The next person I speak to denies my claim for interim housing because of some exception on my insurance plan, blah blah, and I want to scream. I don't, but it's simmering dangerously close to the surface.

I place a few more calls and argue my case, but I'm denied.

Denied.

Denied.

Eventually, I give in to the hopelessness, hanging up the phone that Hank gave me. It's been a real lifesaver. I should find a way to thank him—something that won't give him the wrong idea, though.

Now I finally have access to my money, but it'll be a while before I get my insurance settlement, so I have to pay for replacing everything in the meantime that I need to keep doing my job. After blowing my limited wad on a new tablet and computer, I try to set up a desk in the corner of Sandra's living room. But the house is small and cramped as it is, and we're always in each other's way.

Of course, we have fun times together, watching movies late into the night and eating food that's bad for us to try to forget about the fire. It reminds me of when we were teenagers and snuck a small television into our room to watch bad late-night TV.

But even when she's too tired to get up and be a busybody, Sandra is constantly interrupting my work to ask for things. I don't mind helping, but it was easier to focus on my job when I lived elsewhere and only came over when she needed me.

She's feeling better these days, which is good, and I try to hold that one upside close. But it also means she's up more often, *tsk*ing as she cleans around me. I wake up to find the clothes I dropped on the floor folded and placed on the chair. Everything is put away and rearranged, like some fairy came in the middle of the night.

This is why we live in separate places, in separate homes. As much as I love her, at some point, this will escalate. She'll shoot me dirty looks when I don't put something back exactly where it belongs and exclaim loudly when she finds something out of place.

But I don't have a choice right now about my sleeping arrangement, so I do my best to abide by her strict guidelines and not leave anything out on the counters. From time to time, I think about Hank's offer of the spare room, and wonder why I didn't accept. When my debit card arrives, I go to buy some new clothes, and get a little organizer to put against the wall so they're not lying around.

Then I leave a half-finished muffin out, intending to come back to it later, and I hear Sandra grumbling about ants as she tosses it in the trash.

"That was mine," I grouch as she dumps it.

"Don't leave food out. Put it in a container."

It's barely a few weeks into cohabitating when I'm already so close to exploding I could scream. That's the last thing I want to do when things are already fragile between

Sandra and me, so instead, I get up out of my chair, throw on a coat, and head out into the spring afternoon air.

"Where are you going?" my sister calls.

"Out." And then I slam the door behind me.

I breathe in as much fresh oxygen as I can, grateful for it filling my lungs. I coughed up dark stuff for a few days after the fire, and I never want to go through that again.

I head down the street, and it's not until I'm standing right outside that I realize I've walked to Hank's house. It's cute and surprisingly big, with a porch that has two chairs, a little table, a barbecue grill, and some children's toys scattered around the yard—among them a plastic slide and a forgotten Big Wheel.

I puzzle over it for a while, these remnants of the little boy who lives here. My son. My flesh and blood child.

"Who's that lady, Dad?" a little voice says.

I glance up to find Hank coming down the street, holding the hand of a small minotaur child. The boy is patterned just like his father, splotched all white and brown.

But his eyes... his eyes aren't anything like Hank's, which are big and endless and brown. No, the boy's eyes are bright blue.

Just like mine.

"Milo?" I ask reflexively. The boy's eyebrows jump high into his shaggy hair. He really needs a haircut. I can barely make out the nubs of his horns through it.

"How does she know my name?" The minotaur boy tilts his head at me. "I don't know her."

"I know her," Hank says gently, leading him toward me. Milo is studying me as they come to a stop. "She is, um... a friend of mine."

"Ohh." Milo nods like this is all information that he knows already. "Is she coming in? Can she meet Darla?" He drops his father's hand and comes over to me, grabbing onto my pant leg and tugging me in the direction of his house. "Darla likes other girls. Did you know my dad is bringing home a baby from the baby factory? But we don't know if it'll be a boy or a girl." He continues on like a freight train. "I hope it's a girl, though. So Darla will be happier."

I glance up at Hank with a brow raised. "Baby factory, huh?" I ask. "That's lucky. That there are factories for babies."

Hank drags a hand down his long face in embarrassment.

"I don't think Phoebe needs to meet Darla today," Hank says, prying Milo's hands off me and taking them into his own huge palms.

"Oh." Milo looks vastly disappointed by this.

"But we were going to play some *Monster Masher*, right?" Hank pinches the boy's furry cheek. "Do you want to go get it set up? We can order pizza tonight."

Milo's eyes get big and round, his eyebrows lifting. I'm startled by how much this expression reminds me of myself.

"*Pizza?*" he exclaims, and I'm promptly forgotten. He rushes headlong into the house, his tiny tail flicking wildly behind him as his little hooves gallop up the steps. Then he vanishes inside.

"I should, um, probably go," Hank says awkwardly, hovering like he wants to go after Milo.

Oh, right. I'm just on a walk, and I'm creeping around his house.

"Yeah, of course. I hope you guys have a fun night playing *Monster Masher*."

Hank hesitates, biting his lip with one of his big, square molars like he's thinking hard.

"Do you want some pizza?" he finally asks. "If you don't want to, I understand. No pressure, or—"

Before I can think twice about it, I answer, "Yes."

Why? Why did I say that? Because I wanted to. Because the last thing I want right now is to walk back to my sister's house, and instead, the lights are on inside Hank's cute two-story suburban home, warm and waiting.

And Milo. Who is he? *What* is he?

Hank's eyes light up like the sun. He grins widely, and gestures for me to walk on ahead of him, in through the open front door.

Who knows what I'll find on the other side?

eleven

HANK

She actually agreed. She's coming inside my house. She's going to spend time with Milo and me, and I think my heart just might explode out of my chest as she steps through the front door.

"Pizza! Pizza!" Milo is calling out as he races into the living room, then around through the entryway back to the kitchen again.

"Shh," I tell him, picking up my phone. "I have to order it first." I glance at Phoebe, who's standing in the entryway like she's not sure where to go or what to do with herself. "Sit down, if you like. Water? Soda?" I start putting together a pizza order, then stop. "What do you like on your pizza?"

She looks like a deer in the headlights. "Um…"

Milo sprints into the room again. "Pepperoni! Double pepperoni!"

I don't miss the fond smile that Phoebe has on her face as she watches him blaze past.

"Double pepperoni is fine with me," she says gamely. "Can we get those breadsticks, though? I love them."

I'm surprised—and more than pleased—that she would ask.

"Of course. I've even got some rewards points to spend." We probably order pizza more often than we should, but who's going to stop me? Milo knows not to talk to Grandma about how much we eat pizza.

Once I've got the order placed, I offer to show Phoebe around the house. Yeah, maybe it's a little bit so that she can see the guest room. I don't know how she's been enjoying staying on her sister's couch, but I imagine it gets awkward after a while. If anything, I'd say Phoebe looks stiffer than the last time I saw her.

Or maybe she's just really uncomfortable here.

"Will you give her a tour?!" Milo asks. "Dad, can we show her my bedroom?"

Phoebe grins at him. "I'd love to see your room."

I pat his head. "Of course you can show her."

Milo darts into the living room first, where Darla is sitting on the arm of the couch, sleeping. He rushes over to her, then gently pats her head.

"This is Darla," he tells Phoebe with great importance. "She talks to me sometimes."

Phoebe shoots me a surprised look.

"You can pet her," Milo allows. Obediently, Phoebe pets Darla on the head, and the cat leans into her touch. Milo *oohs*. "She likes you," he says, nodding firmly. "She just told me."

I thought I was giving the tour, but I fall backseat to Milo, who drags Phoebe down the hall to show her the bathroom and the garage. Then we're headed up the stairs, and Milo makes a beeline for his room.

"This is mine!" he shouts proudly.

His room is kind of a mess, and I'm embarrassed for Phoebe to see it. I've always believed that my kid's space is his space, and though I try to encourage him to keep it neat and put his clothes away, they still end up all over the floor.

"Here. This is my ant farm." He pulls Phoebe by the hand across the room to his desk, where the ant farm is busy, as always. "That one's Hambone, that's Cupcake, and that one is, uh…"

He gives up pointing out each of the ants, then hops out of his chair and gestures to his bed, which is covered in spaceships.

"I'm going to be an astronaut," he declares, patting the comforter. "I'm learning how to hold my breath so I can be good at it."

Phoebe furrows her brow at this, but eventually smiles and nods. "Very important for astronauts," she says as Milo heads back out the door.

Unfortunately, he decides to visit my room next. The idea of Phoebe seeing it sends prickles up my back. I'm not messy by any stretch, but it feels… personal. I can imagine her there too easily, on my bed, lying naked on her back.

Milo pushes the door open, and I have no reason to hide it, so I let him. He peeks in and then gestures for Phoebe to follow. She gives me a questioning arch of her eyebrow.

"It's all right," I mouth to her.

My room is dark, as I often have to sleep during the day to be ready for my shifts. Milo hops onto my bed and jumps on it. "I sleep here sometimes!"

"Don't bounce on the bed," I call, and he quickly stops.

"Just when I'm scared, though," Milo says, patting his little chest. "Not as much as I used to."

Standing here with Phoebe so close, the scent of her shampoo in my nose... I wonder what it would be like to be alone with her. To push her down on that bed, surround her with my arms, and actually kiss her like I almost did at the hospital.

Then we're off to the next room, and I thank my lucky stars for Milo's short attention span.

"This is for the baby," Milo says as we reach the last door to the guest room. He bounds inside, spinning around in a circle next to the bed. "We're going to decorate it, right, Dad?"

I nod and smile. "Of course. We'll pick out some nice colors and paint the walls."

"Can we do dinosaurs?"

I rub my chin thoughtfully. "What if the baby doesn't like dinosaurs?"

Milo gasps in indignation. "*Everyone* likes dinosaurs." He shoots Phoebe a suspicious look. "You like dinosaurs, don't you?"

She grins. "My favorite is Argentinosaurus. I mean, it was the biggest animal to ever live. Pretty amazing, huh?"

I cock my head. The woman knows her dinosaurs.

Milo squeals. "Totally amazing! But I like velociraptors better. They had feathers, did you know?"

He prattles on about dinosaurs as we leave behind the guest room, but I catch Phoebe glance back over her shoulder at it. Maybe there's still a chance.

After Milo's shown Phoebe the upstairs bathroom and the crawl space, the doorbell rings.

"Pizza!" he howls, sprinting for the door.

Once we've secured the pizza, I spread it out on the table and we help ourselves. Phoebe eats almost all the breadsticks by herself. When we're finished, she starts hastily cleaning up our plates.

"I'll take care of it later, don't worry," I say, and she pauses mid-collection.

"Are you sure?"

"Yeah. It's fine."

She lets out a heavy sigh, and I can't tell if it's despondence or relief.

"What's wrong?" I ask as Milo bounces to the living room to set up *Monster Masher*.

"Oh, it's just..." Phoebe massages her temples. "My sister. Everything in her house has to be *just so*. Use a plate, put it in the dishwasher right away or get scolded. Don't leave out your snack. Make sure everything goes back where it belongs the moment you use it."

Now I understand. "That sounds rough. Constantly walking on eggshells."

"It's so tiring! Sometimes you just want to put a plate in the sink and deal with it later, you know?"

I laugh. "I know. I usually wait to do all the chores until Milo's asleep."

A small smile crosses Phoebe's mouth. "He's cute," she says in a much quieter voice. "He has so much energy."

"All the time, all day, every day," I say with a groan, and she giggles. It's fucking adorable, her giggle, and oh how I want to make her giggle again.

"He kicked a lot." Phoebe looks thoughtful. "I guess I'm not surprised."

"Dad!" Milo calls from the other room. "I'm picking my character!"

"Don't take Cerberus," I call back. "You know that's mine."

"Aw! But who will Phoebe play?"

I glance at her, not sure if she's prepared to stay any longer. "You're welcome to go whenever you need," I tell her so he can't hear. "It's not a problem."

She rapidly shakes her head. "No, I'm having fun. Let's go play the game."

I can't help a dumb grin as she makes her way into the living room after Milo. Maybe this could go better than I expected.

PHOEBE

Milo is beyond "cute." He's precious and adorable and quick as a whip for being only five. He talks like he's much older. When he wins a game, he jumps to his feet and spins around in a circle, which he calls his "purra-purra victory dance," whatever that means. He utterly destroys me at the fighting game, even when I pick the supposedly "strongest" character to play. I can tell that Hank lets him win when they square off, but puts up a reasonable fight so Milo thinks he's earned it.

And Hank. He smells so utterly fantastic, just like in the breeding room. He gives his son such soft, sweet smiles when otherwise he's rather reserved, and it makes my chest squeeze tight.

It's not long, though, before Milo starts dozing off. While Hank and I are playing a round of *Monster Masher* together, Milo passes out cold on the couch, leaning against Hank's arm.

"I guess it's time for bed," Hank says quietly, then scoops up the little minotaur in his muscular arms. God, he's ripped. Strong and built like a truck, and the flexing of his pectorals and biceps under his tank top make me squirm in my seat.

I let him go upstairs alone, and play a few rounds against a computer opponent while I wait for him to come back. I really should leave now, but I'm not ready to go home and face Sandra, not yet. This was such a welcome break from the stress of the fire that I want to stay in this protective bubble as long as possible.

That spare room... I can't help thinking how welcoming it looked, how comfortable it would be to stay somewhere I have my own space, where I'm not constantly being watched and judged. I could sleep past six, maybe, and use the little desk in the corner to work and be left alone. And it's just down the block, so I could easily scoot over to Sandra's to cook meals and take care of her like I always do.

I can't believe I'm thinking like this. Hank is a complete unknown to me. It would make no sense to move in with him. I've only just met Milo. And even if I did live here, could I really expect nothing untoward to happen? Hank and I have a history. He's the father of the baby I'm carrying. My whole body sizzles at the idea of having something more with him, and that in itself frightens me.

It all sounds too reasonable, and I can't fall in love with Hank Pittsfield. Aside from my responsibilities to Sandra, what would we tell Milo? How could I possibly admit to that little boy who I really am?

I'm not his mother. I may have carried him and given birth to him, but he's not mine. That opens a whole other can of worms.

When Hank comes back, he sits beside me on the couch and picks up the controller. "Another round?"

I nod and agree, hoping to draw out my time with him just a little longer, knowing this shouldn't happen again. This is innocent enough, playing video games together, even if I'm terrible at it. Hank tries to give me some tips, but it's like trying to teach a dog to speak. Eventually I give up, tossing the controller onto the ottoman. Hank laughs.

"Just takes practice," he says. "You're welcome to come over and play with us anytime."

We're on dangerous ground already. This handsome guy, who makes an amazing dad, who knows how to have fun, who keeps his house tidy but not impeccable like Sandra... it would be too easy to trip over the line and get in too deep.

But I can't have DreamTogether find out. And I don't have room in my life for all of this, for the complicated tangle of feelings this promises to be. I already got over Hank Pittsfield once, five years ago, and I don't want to have to get over him again when it doesn't work out.

"Yeah..." I say, trailing off. "I don't know if I should come over a second time."

Hank's face falls, and his shoulders draw together. "Oh. I see." He looks down at me with big, brown eyes, and it would be delightfully simple to just drown in them. To drown in them, and then drown in *him* the way I did at DreamTogether.

"That's too bad," Hank finally says, glancing away with his ears pinned back. "Milo really liked you."

"It's just..." I take a deep breath. "I liked him, too. I liked him a lot. And, I, uh..." Fuck. Can I really say it? Should I say it? "And I really like you, too. Which is so, so complicated, Hank."

I hope he can understand what I'm trying to get across,

because I don't have the words for it: that if I spend more time with him, I'm going to fall head over heels for him. And if I do that, that means falling for Milo, too, and then what?

I have too many things on my plate. I have work, and I have Sandra, and I have this baby growing inside me. Anonymity was crucial in the contract I signed to be a surrogate, and DreamTogether's legal team is pretty clear about breaching that contract.

I can't give Hank what he wants. What he *deserves*.

"Why?" he finally asks, turning to face me on the couch and pulling up one of his hooves to tuck it under him. "Why is it complicated?"

I rub the bridge of my nose because I don't want to have to explain this to him.

"Because of DreamTogether. Because I'm pregnant with your kid. Because of who Milo is." I cross my arms, wrapping them protectively around myself. "Because of who you are."

Hank's mouth opens like he's going to say something, but the longer he looks at me, really *looks* at me, seeing inside me... it closes again, and he nods with a sharp exhale of breath.

"I understand." I can tell that saying it is painful for him. "We're a lot to take on."

It's not that I don't want to try—it's not that they're too much. It's that I'm not enough.

"I have so many responsibilities, Hank. I didn't tell you before, but my sister needs a lot of help. Some days she's better and can get around the house, some days she's worse and can't get out of bed at all. I have to work my job and make sure she has what she needs." I dig my fingers into my jeans. "I couldn't give you and Milo the attention you want."

His eyebrows go up. "What do you do for work?"

"Graphic design, illustration. Mostly packaging."

"Oh. That's neat." He frowns. "That does sound like a lot on your shoulders."

I nod as the game music plays in the background. I want to say more, to explain myself, but I'm only going to drive the knife deeper.

"I should go home." I get to my feet. "Sandra will wonder what's happened to me. I was just going on a walk."

Hank offers me a sad smile. "Sorry to derail your walk."

I shake my head rapidly. "No, no. I had a great time. Milo is a really special kid."

My kid. He's half made of me. I carried him, I gave birth to him. I'm sure that's not inconsequential to how I feel about him, how I want to hug him and put him to bed like Hank did, to play video games with him just to see him get excited about winning.

Hank nods in agreement. "He's so much like me sometimes, and then not at all like me." He looks forlorn for a moment. "Those are the parts that are like you, I think."

I don't realize I've been squeezing one of the throw pillows until the seam bites into my hand. I release it, setting it back down on the couch.

"Thank you again," I say quickly, then head for the front door. Hank follows me, and I hate the kicked-puppy look on his face. "Hope I see you around soon."

He just nods. "It was my pleasure. Really." As I step out, he adds, "The room is still available for you, if you ever need it. And I wouldn't... expect anything."

The temptation is strong. But wouldn't it be painful, too, to sleep down the hall from this handsome minotaur, who's so kind and sweet and is such a good father? I know I can't have anything more with him, and in such close proximity, could I really stay away?

It would just be torture. So I shake my head and say, "I appreciate the offer, Hank, but I can't. Have a good night."

Walking out the door feels like turning my back on something wonderful—something too wonderful for me to have.

Hank stands on the porch, leaning against the doorframe with resigned acceptance on his face.

"Good night, Phoebe."

twelve

PHOEBE

WHEN I STEP INSIDE SANDRA'S HOUSE, I FIND HER SITTING ON the couch with all my pillows and blankets neatly folded and arranged on the chair. The TV is on and her knitting is in her lap, but she looks half asleep.

"Where have you been?" she says, sitting up abruptly. "You were gone for a long time."

"Sorry." I sit down beside her, collapsing into the sinking cushions. "I didn't mean to. I just... got sucked in."

"By what? Did you go down to the park and end up playing on the merry-go-round?"

I drop my head in my hands. "No. Hank."

"Hank?" Sandra puts an arm around my shoulders, squeezing me. "Tell me everything."

So I do, from seeing the spare bedroom to the awkward conversation we had at the end of the night. Her brows draw further and further together as I talk.

"He has an extra room? And he offered it to you?" She cocks her head. "That's not a bad idea, Feebs. I mean, you're literally pregnant with his kid. Maybe it would be a good thing. You'd have your own space until your house is built, and the dad would be right there if anything comes up."

I gape at her. "What? It would be idiotic of me to move in with him. We're not dating, for starters. We barely know each other."

Sandra waggles her eyebrows. "Really, though? You've been fucked senseless by him a few times, if I remember right."

"That's the problem!" I could just scream. "I want it to happen again! He's hot, Sandra. He's really, really hot. And sweet. And soft-spoken. And he loves Milo so, so much." I try to steel my voice against cracking, but I can't help it as I remember Hank carrying a sleeping Milo up the stairs. "But we can't have a relationship."

"Why not?" Sandra asks, genuinely perplexed.

"For starters, I'd be violating the contract. DreamTogether could *not* find out. I would lose this job." Just the thought of it sends a tremor through me. "Besides, who would I be in that situation if I started dating Hank? I'm not some random lady off the street. I'm Milo's *mom*, for fuck's sake."

"Are you, though?" she asks. "You're an egg donor, really. You never met him, not since he was born."

I guess she's right. I'm only Milo's biological mother. I didn't partake at all in raising him.

"Maybe it's not as complicated as you think," Sandra says. "You guys don't have to tell him the truth, not immediately. You'll have a place to stay, and then when the house is done, you can just move out. It's only temporary."

"It could take ages," I argue. "A lot could happen in that time if I'm *living* with him. The second I start to show, we're going to have to explain everything. And then what? I can't be a parental figure to that kid, Sandra. Or to this baby. I can't have that kind of life."

"I don't understand why you think that."

"I already have so much on my plate! I have my job, Sandra. I have DreamTogether. And I have—"

I cut myself off.

I have you.

We both stare at each other as the invisible words still come out. I didn't mean to say it.

"Oh." With a sigh, Sandra picks herself up off the couch with some effort. "Well, next time, just send me a text message to tell me where you are."

Then she hobbles off to bed, and I'm left on the couch feeling like the biggest asshole possible.

HANK

I understand so much more now that Phoebe's told me everything. She is a complicated woman, and it only makes me like her more. She has so many layers to peel back, and high protective walls around a good, loving heart.

She was adorably awkward but natural with Milo, and I saw the look in her eyes when she played with him. Sure, he's not lacking in charm, but there was something even more tender there. She can feel what I feel when I look at him: the pieces of myself and the pieces of her, bundled up together into a mysterious little package, one that promises endless new surprises. Could she see all the threads of herself woven through him, into a new creature with his own mind, and emotions, and empathy, that now we can watch bloom?

After flicking off the lights, I lock up and head to my room. Instantly I remember Phoebe standing in here, and the scent of her lingers in the air. All I have to do is think that errant thought again about her on my bed, fully naked and looking up at me, and my cock slips from its sheath, growing steadily under my jeans.

No. I'm not going to gratify it. Fantasizing about Phoebe's soft cries, her little moans as I fucked her on the bench, won't help me get over her. And that might be what I have to do.

Instead, I turn on the shower, leaving the water cold, and step in. It sends a shock down my back, straight to my balls. I pant under the onslaught and still, I'm imagining her. Now that I've seen her face, now that I've watched her laugh and almost cry, it's easy to picture what Phoebe's face would look like while I was inside of her.

But we wouldn't be hurried along like we were at Dream-Together. No, I'd take my time with her, weighing her down to the bed under me, thrusting into her over and over until she's open enough to take my entire cock. I would wring the pleasure out of her, one orgasm after another, in every possible position.

And I could look into her limitless blue eyes while I did it.

Finally, I have no choice but to pump one out. And damn, it feels great, too, despite the freezing water. In my mind, my hand becomes Phoebe's absolutely flawless pussy, squeezing and pulsing as she writhes under me. Now she's saying my name, calling it out into the sky while I show her what kind of life she could have with me.

It only takes me seconds to finish, and my cum sprays

out, shooting across the shower to land on the tile in a massive splooge.

Damn. I've jerked off a lot of times thinking about Phoebe, but not quite like that.

Something about tonight, about seeing her so unguarded with Milo, makes me crave her in an even deeper, more fearsome way. A hidden, darker part of me emerges, demanding that she be *here*, where we both know she belongs.

"Hank!"

I didn't sleep much last night, consumed with the thought of how I'm going to convince Phoebe to move in with Milo and me, so I've been sitting at the dining room table with a mug of coffee in my hand. I jolt upright at the sound of my mother's voice.

"Hank! Hank! I won!" She comes bounding into the kitchen with more energy than I think I've ever seen her have.

"You won what?" I ask, rubbing my eyes. I think I was falling asleep at the table.

Milo comes in soon after. "Grandma is going to Bahama-mamas!" he says. "Right, Grandma? That's what they said!"

I squint at my mother. "The Bahamas? How?"

"I won!" she repeats, as if this explains it. "On the radio! I called in during trivia hour and answered the question correctly. I was caller number one hundred, so I won!"

"So... you're going?" I ask cautiously. "When?"

"Whenever I want!" She hoots. "I don't think I've had a vacation since Milo was born."

Ah, shit. I know it's not been the easiest for her, helping

me take care of him. But she's always been happy to do it, so I never even considered what an inconvenience it might be to her personal life.

"Sorry," she mutters when she realizes what she's said.

"No, no. It's true." I grunt with exhaustion. Milo has long since moved on, walking around Darla in circles in the living room chanting, "Bahama-mamas." I gaze up at my mother, whose hair and fur have been graying for some time, and who has new lines around her eyes and muzzle that she's only developed in the last few years. We go to the beach from time to time, and have even stayed the night before, but vacations with Milo are still a lot of work.

"You should go, Mom," I tell her earnestly. "I can find a nanny to help in the meantime, and I have a few days of vacation saved up." This isn't completely true, but I can get some of my coworkers to swap shifts with me.

She eyes me with suspicion. "Are you sure? Milo's never had someone else for an extended period of time."

As we speak, I'm going through my mental rolodex. I'll need someone who can drive Milo to school and pick him up some days. Someone older, who either doesn't have a job or has a flexible one. Perhaps one of Mom's friends?

"I can figure it out," I say, turning on my phone. "Don't worry about us. Go take care of yourself for once."

"If you say so..." She trails off, then glances out of the side of her eye toward the living room, where Milo is playing with Darla. "What about Phoebe?"

I gape at her. That's an ask I couldn't possibly make, not of Phoebe, and certainly not with everything she already has on her plate. She would turn me down without question.

"She works from home," Mom says, ticking off one finger. "She has a car. She knows Milo already after last night." She waggles her eyebrows at me. So, Milo told her everything. "And she's his mother."

I hold a finger to my mouth and shush her.

"He doesn't know anything," I say in a low voice. "We're keeping it that way until Phoebe wants him to know. *If* she ever wants him to know."

Mom arches an eyebrow. "If?"

"It's complicated."

"Of course it is," she says with sympathy. "But you should still tell him. The longer you wait..."

"I need Phoebe to be comfortable first." My tone is firm. Nothing happens without her say-so.

"Fine." Mom doesn't look all that dissuaded, though. "I'm going next week."

My jaw falls open. "So soon?"

"They said I could use it whenever I want, and next week is my birthday, so..."

I might be the world's worst son right now. I completely forgot. "Oh, of course. Then go."

"Are you sure? You can figure it out before then?"

I bat a hand at her. "I'm not incapable. Go."

Mom allows herself a small smile. "I'll make the reservations," she says, then trots out of the room.

What am I going to do?

PHOEBE

I think I might actually implode.

I haven't had a good night's sleep in what feels like months, though I know it hasn't been that long. The couch digs into my side and my back at all sorts of uncomfortable angles no matter how I lie down or how many blankets I put on it first.

Work has been hell since I went back, too. After losing all my files, I feel like I never have the thing I need at hand, and I'm constantly behind. Finally, I have to tell my boss that I'm going down to four days a week, because I'm just too... tired.

Tired. All the time, and not just because of the lack of sleep. I feel like I'm always being pulled in ten directions at once, trying to pick up the scattered bits of my life and put them together into something resembling familiar. There's insurance to deal with constantly, and I'm already racking up credit card debt. Replacing all of our paperwork has been a nightmare. Sandra tries to help, but she doesn't understand the bureaucracy any better than I do. Sometimes I cry after a bad phone call, and she has to put down her knitting to hug me.

At least she's forgiven me for what I said. But we've always been good at that, as sisters—sure, we've hurt each other, but we've also learned that we're all each other has. At the end of the day, it's just us, trying to survive.

And still, we get on each other's nerves. The house is too small and each of our personalities is too big to fit inside it. Every night on the couch, I think about Hank and Milo, wishing I was there instead.

Fuck. I never should have gone in for pizza that night, seen their cute house, seen how sweetly and wonderfully they interact. It's obvious how much Hank loves that little kid. If I'd had a dad like Hank... things would be different. Maybe I would have had a good example.

But even in our foster home, we never really had a "parent." In our second family, Clarissa was nice enough, but always kept us at arm's length. She didn't want to get attached to us in case we were moved, and we felt the same way.

Milo is a lucky kid, and he deserves people in his life who can give him that kind of undivided attention and love. I am not that person.

And I can't lose my job at DreamTogether, especially now.

I haven't heard from Hank since that night, just like I asked. Still, it sucks. I wish I could hear his deep voice again. I take out the phone he gave me and look him up after I've turned out all the lights, staring at that photo of him in the orange pants, which now I know is from a calendar the fire station did for a charity event.

Explains the topless minotaur.

What would it be like to look into his face while we have sex? This thought occurs to me frequently late at night, and I've masturbated more times than I can count just to that picture.

But my decision not to involve myself with Hank only becomes surer when Sandra takes a turn. These happen sometimes, periods of time where everything is worse, and then she can't get up at all. I work in the living room, listening for her call in case she needs help. We've scheduled doctor's appointments, but they're going to say what they always say: they don't know what's causing it, and they have no answers.

It's about nine o'clock one night, and I'm trying to finish an illustration that's due tomorrow when I get a call from an unrecognized number.

"Hello?" a frantic voice on the other end says, before I can even utter a greeting.

"Hello, this is Phoebe."

"You're Milo's emergency contact?" The woman on the

other end sounds like she's losing it. "Because he's really sick and he's freaking out. I tried to call his dad, but Hank's phone is off—"

"Emergency contact?" I'm trying to think of when Hank ever asked me about that.

"Yes," the woman says. "Your name was on the fridge. Milo won't listen to me. He's babbling nonsense, and I don't know what to do."

I run to the front door and look outside, and sure enough, down the block, someone is standing outside Hank and Milo's house, a hand in her hair as she talks to me on the phone.

If Hank is at work, and Milo's having a crisis...

Fuck.

"I'll be right there," I tell her, and hang up.

HANK

It's been a long, long day.

I'm already exhausted when the alarm goes off a second time, and we all jump into the truck to respond to the call. When we arrive, a woman is on the front lawn on her knees, sobbing. Two of her neighbors, an elderly couple, are holding her back from running into the building.

After hearing there are still two children inside, Ron and I move as one. I bludgeon down the door, and he rushes past me. He sprints up the stairs straight into the flames, while I charge down the downstairs hallway.

I hear screaming through an open doorway. Inside, a human boy is curled up in his bed.

I sweep him off it in one motion, taking the blanket with me so I can throw it over him.

"Cover your eyes," I tell him, then wrap my arms all the way around his little body and charge back out the door.

Ron is successful in bringing down the older girl who lived there, too, but she has minor burns and injuries from smoke inhalation. We stand with them and their mother as the ambulance pulls up.

By the time we're back at the station and I can check my phone again, it's been nearly four hours.

"Hi, Hank, it's Phoebe," my voicemail says, and I stop in my tracks. Her voice is eerily calm. "I'm with Milo right now. He's fine. Please call me back when you can."

I play the next voicemail. "Hank! It's Janelle, and Milo is... he's really upset. He's sweating and throwing up, and I don't know what to do—"

I hear Milo in the background crying, and all the hair on my body stands on end.

Wait. Think. It takes a moment before I understand this turn of events. Phoebe's message is last—which means that for whatever reason, the sitter called Phoebe to come help.

After throwing my gear in my locker, I'm still tugging on my shirt when I rush out of the station and get in the car.

Milo.

thirteen

PHOEBE

Janelle is surprised and relieved at my sudden appearance. She leads me inside to find Milo on the couch, the fur on his forehead slick with sweat. When Janelle kneels in front of him to tell him that I've arrived, he starts crying and pushes her away.

"Dad!" he whimpers, reaching out toward nothing.

I stroke him over the blanket. "Hey, Milo. It's me."

His eyes finally seem to register that I'm there, and his frantic thrashing stops.

"Phoebe!" He tries to sit up, but he can't, his body swaying as he lies back down. "I feel so bad. Everything is pink." The rest of the words that come out of his mouth are garbled.

"I think he's running a fever," Janelle says as I rummage around the downstairs bathroom. I find a thermometer and verify her suspicion.

"Fudge. It's 103.5." That's much too high. "We have to take him to a hospital."

"A hospital?!" The poor woman is horrified. "Hank's going to kill me."

I shake my head and pick Milo up off the couch, staggering under his weight. He isn't just a little five-year-old human boy—he is a *minotaur* boy, and I need a wheelbarrow for him.

Janelle helps me carry him out to the car as he whimpers and moans. At least she has a medical release from Hank just in case of an emergency like this, so she comes with me to be his guardian.

One fever reducer and some IV fluids later, the hospital staff helps us carry Milo back to the car. At the house, we bring him inside together, but unfortunately, we can't get him up the stairs, so we lay him on the couch with his head on my lap.

After the frazzled Janelle leaves, I sit there stroking Milo's shaggy hair, watching the even breaths he lets out of his cute, round muzzle. I adjust the blanket laid across him to keep him warmer.

From here, I can see into the kitchen. And sure enough, there is a note on the refrigerator that reads:

MILO EMERGENCY CONTACT

PHOEBE

With the phone number of the phone he gave me listed underneath. And frankly, I'm glad it was me, though I can't say I ever gave permission for it to go there.

All's well that ends well. I lean my head back against the soft couch with its new, plush cushions, and my eyes fall closed. Milo's soft fur under my hand lulls me to sleep.

"Phoebe?!" I jerk awake at the sound of Hank's worried voice. He comes into the room, and his brown eyes are big and wide, his breath harried.

"Shh." I hold up a finger to my lips as Milo stirs, then offer him a smile. "It's okay. He's all right now. But we should keep an eye on him."

With a sigh of relief, Hank sinks into the chair next to the couch. His face is sooty, and he looks absolutely exhausted.

"What a fucking day," he murmurs, his head falling back. "What on earth happened? How did you get mixed up in this?"

I blink at him. "What do you mean? My name was on the fridge, clearly labeled 'Milo's emergency contact.'" I shoot him a chastising look. "You could have told me first, at least."

His head jerks up. "I never did that."

"It's on the fridge. In the kitchen."

Getting out of the chair, he heads into the next room and spies the same thing I did. Then, a realization seems to strike him, and he rolls his eyes. "My mother."

"Your mother?"

He returns, sinking even deeper into the chair this time as he rubs his face. "She did that. Meddling. I'm sorry."

"I'm glad Janelle called me," I say, stroking Milo's head. "He has a fever, and he was starting to hallucinate. He calmed down when I got here, though, and we took him to the hospital."

Hank stiffens all over. "The hospital?"

"The fever broke pretty quickly, but they sent home some more of that strong fever reducer in case it gets bad again."

His mouth slightly ajar, he nods in understanding.

"Thank you," he says, voice turning hoarse. "You really went above and beyond."

I swallow the words I want to say, that he's my son, too,

and it's the bare minimum I can do for him. Instead, I say, "I was in the right place at the right time. Anyway, what happened to you tonight? You were AWOL for a long time."

He looks fully exhausted as he says, "Two fires. Two families that have lost everything." His kind eyes find mine, and they're full of sorrow. "The second one was a single mom and her two kids. The girl almost didn't get out—she wouldn't have without Ron. So when I got that voicemail..." Hank trails off, clearly too rattled to even say the words.

"Everything is fine." I risk leaning forward to put a hand on his shoulder, and at first, he tenses up under me. Then, his muscles all seem to release at once, and he sags forward. He puts his other hand on mine and squeezes it.

"The moment I heard your voice, I knew it would be all right." He stares down at the floor. "I knew Milo would be safe with you. That you would do what needs to be done."

"I guess I'm glad your mom put my name on the fridge," I say. "Janelle was scared out of her mind."

He shakes his head. "She was my only option when Mom went out of town."

I know why he didn't call me instead. Still, it would be fun to spend that much time with Milo. I want to learn everything about him.

"How much longer is your mom gone?" I definitely don't trust Janelle to look after Milo anymore. He needs someone he feels comfortable with.

Hank cocks an eyebrow. "Another three days."

So Saturday, Sunday, and Monday. I try not to work over the weekend when possible, and I can probably take Monday off.

I can't believe I'm thinking about offering this, but I don't like the idea of Milo being stuck with another stranger. If Hank has no other options...

"What if I looked after him?" I ask. "Maybe he doesn't know me that well yet, but he trusted me when he was scared. I think that's a good sign."

Hank's head jerks up, and his mouth falls open.

"You would?" He sounds hopeful but hesitant. "Really?"

I hope I'm not sending him the wrong message, but it seems like he's really in a pickle here, and I can help.

"I'm right down the street. It doesn't make sense for you to pay someone else to do it."

"Well, I would pay you—"

Just the thought of it makes my skin crawl. "No." I clear my throat, then look down at Milo's sleeping face in my lap, and my heart squeezes. "It would be my pleasure to spend some time with him."

"You'd have to pick him up from school..." Hank trails off.

"So? I'll say I'm his nanny. Write me a note."

"Only if you're sure." He scratches one of his cute little ears, and opens his mouth like he's about to say something more, but thinks better of it.

"I'm sure," I say with surprising confidence. It'll give me a great opportunity to get out of my sister's house for a while. "Actually, could I hang out here while he's at school? So I can get some work done?"

Hank blinks those long-lashed eyes. "Oh. Yeah, of course. You can do whatever you want." The hint of a smile pulls at his lips. "My house is your house."

That sounds a little more serious than I was thinking, but I thank him anyway.

I gently set Milo's head down on a pillow where I was sitting and get to my feet. "All right, now that you're home, I should probably go."

Hank walks with me to the front door. When I step out, he follows me and shuts it behind him.

"Thank you again," he says with a heavy swallow. "I really don't know what I, or Milo, would have done without you tonight. I'm sorry about my mom getting you involved." Hank's eyes are moist, though, and I think this has all thoroughly shaken him. His son means the world to him, that much is obvious, and the adrenaline of worrying hasn't worn off.

"It's okay. I was happy to do it." I pat his arm. "His safety means a lot to me, too."

Hank gazes down at me, then suddenly, he wraps both his big arms around me and pulls me in for a hug. My cheek is crushed against his chest as he squeezes me. He smells like smoke, but also like *him*—a warm, sweet smell that fills me up and calms my heart.

Any instinct I had to pull away vanishes, and I melt into those furry arms that are wrapped so tightly around me. Hank rests his head on mine and holds me like I'm going to disappear.

"Thank you," he murmurs. "Thank you, Phoebe."

HANK

Finally, I realize I ought to release Phoebe, even though she still hasn't spoken. When I free her from my arms, her cheeks are pink and her eyes are glossy. She looks up at me, and for once, she's unguarded.

"Well," she says in a high-pitched voice as she pulls away from me, tripping over her feet. "I should go."

Then she's gone, trotting off down the street back to her sister's house. I watch her, my arms still warm where I held her, my chest aching.

I don't know if that was the right thing to do, but right then, I couldn't help myself. The way she felt protective of Milo made my heart swell and my stomach do somersaults. She knew what needed to be done, and she did it.

My bull's vision homes in on her as she jogs down the street, and I let out a powerful huff before heading inside. The way I need this woman is soul-crushing.

But her agreeing to help me with Milo for the next few days... that gives me hope, too. Maybe I can have what I want if I continue the course.

My poor little calf continues to sweat through the night, tossing and turning and occasionally calling out for me. I end up taking Milo to my room so he can sleep in my bed and I can keep a better eye on him.

By morning, I'm exhausted, but he's got enough energy to shake me awake.

"Daddy," he says. "Phoebe came over last night. She took me to the hospital."

"I know, squirt," I tell him, yawning. "She told me." I try to rub the sleep out of my face. "Seems you like her."

Milo's bright blue eyes are simply glowing. "Yeah! She's quiet, but she feels really big things."

It takes me a second to understand, but I think I agree with him. "She does, doesn't she?"

Phoebe has a tough exterior, but I know she's soft on the inside. It's just one of the many traits I've come to admire about her.

I have to go to work again that afternoon, so I call Phoebe to give her my schedule. She shows up at the front door two hours later with a backpack on, ready to take over. I show her what I had planned for dinner, and she assures me she can cook some pasta without too much direction. The confidence with which she takes control, pouring a cup of water and carrying it while she goes to find Milo in his bedroom, gives me a tingly feeling. He's awake, playing his handheld game in bed, but he tosses it aside when Phoebe walks into the room with me right behind her.

"Remember how I said Phoebe was going to look after you today?" I ask. Milo nods furiously. "Okay. You're sick, so try to take it easy." I kiss his forehead and rub the rounded stubs of his horns for good luck before backing away.

Phoebe waves me off. "No need to hover. You can go to work now. Milo and I will be fine. Right?" She ruffles his hair and he giggles.

They look so natural together that my heart goes wild in my ribcage.

"All right. I'll be back around three in the morning." I nod at Phoebe. "Feel free to use the guest room."

She nods and waves me off, so I see myself out, a great weight off my chest.

Whatever happens, I know Milo's safe with her.

fourteen

PHOEBE

MILO GETS TIRED AGAIN QUICKLY AND FALLS ASLEEP WITH HIS game on his face, so I make sure to save it before setting it on his bedside table.

Then I get to work in complete silence and peace. I accomplish as much as I can before Milo wakes up, and the time flies by. Something about Hank's kitchen is so comforting, with its yellow walls and big front window, the cupboards all painted white. It's easy to see myself working at this table all day.

I'm lost in doodling when I hear a little voice ask, "What are ya doing?"

Milo comes into the kitchen, dressed in his pajamas. He crawls up onto the chair next to mine and peers at my tablet screen. "Whoa. You're drawing on a computer?"

I laugh. "Yep. Cool, huh?" I save my project and open a new, blank document. Then I start doodling something, and his eyes grow into saucers.

"That's amazing." He reaches for the pen, so I slide the tablet closer to him and hand him the stylus.

"Be gentle with it," I tell him, mimicking how I use the stylus. With great care, Milo draws a circle on the screen and lets out a pleased giggle. He experiments with it some more, drawing doodles that, shockingly, resemble the objects they're supposed to be.

"You can even change the colors, too," I tell him, using the stylus to select a different brush and palette. "Here, now it's blue."

He draws a squiggle, and his mouth forms a perfect O.

"Wow," he says with great reverence as he gives the stylus back. "I want one."

"Maybe someday."

We pull out his coloring books and notepads and sit side by side at the table, Milo drawing while I work. We're both silent for nearly an entire hour, focused as we are, and it's not until I glance at him from the side of my eye that I see for the first time what *I* must look like from the outside: hunched over my art, shoulders at an angle that's probably not good for me, focused entirely and completely on the page. He's drawn the same character over and over again, improving the shape and colors a little each time he repeats the drawing.

"Who is that?" I ask, and my question startles him out of his focus. "Sorry. Didn't mean to interrupt your flow."

He shakes his head and looks down at the drawing. "This is Darla as Spider-Man's cat." Once he says it, I can kind of see it: a cat wearing a red and black spider outfit.

His eyes dart over to the screen of my tablet, where I've been drawing a tree that will become the corner of the advertisement. He points at it. "You drew that?"

"Yep."

"That's really good." He gazes down at his own drawing. "Mine's ugly, though."

"Do you want feedback?" I ask.

His brow just furrows in confusion. "I don't think it's time for Darla's dinner yet."

I laugh, and this makes him frown even deeper. "No, no. I'm asking if you want advice. Suggestions for how to make it look the way you want."

"Oh." He puzzles for a moment. "Okay."

I open a new canvas on my tablet and start doodling a cat. I point out the shape of the head, the location of the legs relative to the body, how perspective distorts them. I'm not sure how much of it he understands, but afterward, Milo returns to drawing his cat with renewed vigor.

After cooking him dinner and feeding Darla, all of the little boy's limited energy has drained out of him, and I get him to bed just before he passes out cold. I don't think I could get him there alone.

I'm tired but not exhausted, and there's a pleasant, bubbly feeling in my body that I don't recognize as I head down the single block between the houses to bring Sandra the leftovers.

"You're late," she grumps, and I feel bad for not bringing dinner sooner.

"Sorry. It took a while for Milo to go down." I set the baby monitor on the table so we can both hear the little minotaur's breaths back at the house.

"Hank doesn't mind?" she asks.

"No. And I'll know as soon as he wakes up."

"I'm surprised you agreed to watch him."

I purse my lips. What I'm doing—associating so openly with Hank—feels risky. I don't know how DreamTogether might find out, and still, I worry. But the risk feels worth it when I get to spend time with Milo and make Hank's life easier.

"He has a nice house," is all I can think to say. "And Milo... he's a really good kid." I sit down on the couch and lean back into the soft cushion. "Pretty amazing at art already. He loves it."

"A chip off the old block." Sandra finishes her bite of food and glances at me from the corner of her eye. "I'm surprised you got so involved."

"I didn't have a choice. That lady Janelle had no idea what she was doing, taking care of Milo."

My sister arches a brow. "And you do?"

I feel embarrassed heat rush into my face. She's right, really. I have no experience with kids at all. But being with that little minotaur boy feels natural, like I don't even have to try.

"I don't know," I say, throwing up my hands. "It just seemed like the right thing to do."

"It has nothing to do with the crush you have on his dad, right?" Sandra giggles at my pained expression.

Instead of rising to her bait, I get up and do what I can around the house, taking out the trash and recycling, then pushing the bins down to the curb.

"Thanks," Sandra says, pushing her plate aside. I take it to the sink for her and put it in the dishwasher. "You should probably go back in case Milo wakes up." She sighs when I head for the front door. "For what it's worth, I think you're doing the right thing."

"I just don't want to send Hank the wrong message, either."

I glance over my shoulder and find my sister giving me a deadpan look.

"I think you've shut that guy down enough times that he gets the picture."

Feeling guilty, I head back to Hank's house. Down the hall is the guest room, and it's neatly made up, with the fresh scent of detergent in the air.

I flop down on the bed and groan. Wow. This is by far the most comfortable mattress I've ever felt in my life. How long has it been since I slept in a real bed?

It's like my whole body finally relaxes for the first time in a month as I sink deeper, my face vanishing into the pillow. I'm asleep before I've even finished closing my eyes.

HANK

I'm surprised when I get home to find coloring books all over the table, along with what must be Phoebe's work tablet. Dinner was clearly cooked, because the dishes are in the dishwasher but the pans are still dirty. It brings a smile to my lips to remember the conversation Phoebe and I had about her sister, and how sometimes she just wished she could leave the dishes until later.

I'm still full of pep after the energy drink I had earlier in the night, so I clean up the kitchen, imagining how much fun they had while doing art together at the table. When I'm finished, I tiptoe up the stairs and down the hallway, where I'm surprised to find the guest room door ajar. When I push it open with my nose and peer in, a head of blonde hair peeks out of the blankets.

Phoebe's here, and she's sleeping like the dead.

I smile to myself as I draw away from the door, then head to Milo's room to check on him. It means the world to me that she feels comfortable in my home. It's probably too much to hope, but perhaps tomorrow, she'll reconsider my offer to move in.

I think she needs it as much as I do.

I wake sometime in the afternoon to the faint hum of voices downstairs. I'd left my schedule written on the fridge so Phoebe would know when to expect me up, and I'm thrilled to see her again.

When I pop into the kitchen, Phoebe and Milo are standing in front of the stove, Milo up on a footstool so he can reach.

"You tap the shell on the edge of the pan—not too hard, just to crack the shell," Phoebe says.

Milo smashes the egg against the pan, which blows the egg open. Phoebe laughs so loud I'm shocked by it.

"Okay, not like that," she says with infinite patience, and grabs another egg, even though she's now covered in raw yolk. "Try again, but not so hard."

She glances up, finally noticing me in the doorway, and gives me a shy smile. Then she turns back to the egg Milo's just cracked into the pan and fishes some eggshell out of it.

"Sorry," she says, helping Milo off the footstool. "We wanted to surprise you with dinner, but Milo insisted it would be breakfast for you, so we decided to make eggs and toast."

My stomach rumbles in response, and Phoebe and Milo laugh in unison.

Soon, "dinner" is ready, and I have to pick some shells out of my eggs.

Sorry, Phoebe mouths to me.

While she cuts up some of Milo's food, all I can do is watch and admire them. Something about the way she moves, how she looks at him, how I imagine her already growing another one of my calves inside her... I feel warm all over, from my throat straight to my balls.

Fuck, she's beautiful. She's beautiful, and perfect, and everything I've ever wanted in my entire life. All my years have simply been building up to this moment, when I truly saw my future wife for the first time.

That's what she is. She will be—I'm certain of it now. And you know what they say about bulls.

We're stubborn fuckers.

PHOEBE

While I'm watching Milo, I'm rarely back at my sister's house except to make meals and do a few chores. I've taken to sleeping over at Hank's so Milo's not alone, and the break is much needed—for both of us. Already, she seems happier, more cheerful, more fun.

That's when I'm certain of it: we can't live together anymore if we want to preserve our relationship.

Since I can't leave Milo at home alone, I bring him with me when I carry food over to Sandra, and he's adorably shy at first. She doesn't like his bare hooves tromping all over her carpet, but she manages to restrain herself from saying anything despite the dark look she shoots his little feet.

"I'm Sandra," she introduces herself from the couch. "Phoebe's little sister."

Milo approaches uneasily, his hands tucked behind his back. "I'm Milo." He keeps his eyes on the floor, standing very close to me. I didn't realize he had this tentative, shy side because he's never showed it to me before. "My dad is Hank."

Sandra smiles a friendly smile and offers him a seat on the couch while she eats her dinner. She's sweet as she asks him questions about himself, what he likes to do, how he's enjoying kindergarten. Slowly he opens up, and by the end of our visit, he's bouncing around the living room telling Sandra all about Darla.

And I love getting to spend this kind of time with him. He can be too chatty sometimes, but it's cute, like a little train that can't stop moving no matter what gets in the way. He has a creative mind, always dreaming up silly stories about his drawings.

I'm actually quite sad when Hank's mother gets home from the airport and heads over to the house to see Milo. I was enjoying our time, just the two of us. And Hank's still at work, so I'm nervous about meeting her by myself.

What does she think of me? I work at DreamTogether. She knows purely by Milo's existence who I am to Hank, and who he is to me.

Embarrassing.

Milo and I are in the living room watching a cartoon when the door opens, and a singsong voice calls out, "Milo, I'm back!"

Milo leaps off the couch and sprints to the front door. "Grandma!"

I follow him into the entryway, where he's clutching her legs and hugging her. Unlike Hank, who's splotched all over, his mother is mostly brown with only a few small spots of white on her nose and hands. She's graying around her mouth and cheeks, as well as in her brown hair. Her horns are much smaller, and she's dressed in a tropical skirt and blouse.

"How was the Bahama-mamas?" asks Milo, finally releasing her.

"Warm," she says. "Very warm. Grandma had lots and lots of mojitos."

"Mowi-what?"

She just grins down at him. "Grandma had a good time."

When at last her eyes meet mine, I offer her a small wave. "Hi, I'm Phoebe."

She smirks. "I know. Hey, Milo? Why don't you go grab your latest drawings to show me?"

He bounces on his hooves. "Yeah!" Then he runs off up the stairs.

"Thank you for watching him while I was gone," Hank's mother says, offering me her hand. "I'm Imelda, by the way."

I shake it. "It's good to meet you."

We walk into the living room together, where she gestures for me to take a seat. "I heard there was a kerfuffle with the nanny. I'm glad you were there to step in."

I have to laugh. "Because you put my name on the fridge!"

Imelda winks just as Milo comes barreling into the room again, a bunch of papers clutched in his hands. He spreads them out on the coffee table in front of his grandmother and starts showing off his new version of Darla as Spider-Man's cat.

"Oh, wow, this is good, Milo," she says, and she's not just doing kid-sweet-talk voice.

"Phoebe showed me how to do it!" he exclaims. "She's really good at drawing."

Imelda shoots me a curious look. "Is she?"

"I'm a graphic artist and designer," I say. "It's what I do all day."

"I see. What about DreamTogether?"

I bite my lip, because I don't want to talk about this in front of Milo.

He glances up at me. "What's that?"

"It's my other job," I say quickly. "It's, um, how I met your dad."

Before he can ask more questions, Imelda stands up. "All right, Milo. Time to get ready for bed. Have you had a bath yet?"

I cringe. I haven't really given his hygiene as much thought as I should.

He pouts as he says, "No."

"Then go on upstairs and I'll start the water."

Milo stalks away, clearly displeased with this turn of events. "Phoebe was way more fun," he mutters.

I get up, too, and head to the kitchen to pack up my things.

"Stay as long as you want," Imelda says, but now that she's back... there's no reason for me to be here.

"That's okay. I have to go check on my sister." I sling my bag over my shoulder. "It was fun."

"Maybe you can watch him again," Imelda says as I head to the door. "I could use a break sometimes, and he clearly likes you."

I hover with my hand on the knob. I would love to spend more time with Milo, and especially with Milo and Hank.

"Maybe you should reconsider the offer about the spare room," Imelda goes on. "I think it would be really good for

Milo to have you around. I know Hank won't do anything you don't want to do."

The way she says it, like there's a world in which I *would* want to do things with Hank, makes my skin warm. It might also be torture to have to see him day in and day out, and not try to think about how well he took me on the breeding bench—and what it would be like to do it again, maybe even on that big bed of his in that dark bedroom.

Imelda flashes me a look like she knows exactly what I'm thinking.

"I really shouldn't—" I begin.

"Oh, stop it," she says, batting a hand. "It's not doing you any good sleeping on a couch every night when there's a perfectly good room with a bed here."

Without waiting for my answer, she ushers me out the door.

"Goodnight," I tell her.

"Call Hank tomorrow," she says in answer. Then she shuts it behind me.

fifteen

HANK

When I get off work that night, I have a text message from Phoebe waiting for me.

> Does the offer of the spare room still stand?

My heart leaps—no, it fucking *flies*—into my throat. Hastily I text out an answer, even though it's the middle of the night and she's probably asleep.

> Yes, it does.

She wants to live with us. Even if it's just in a roommate capacity, she wants to live. With. Us.

Milo and I. In our house. In the spare room.

Damn. I get a boner in the car just thinking about it. It's going to be tough to keep my hands to myself, but I will until she's ready.

If she's ever ready. But I shake that thought off. No, I'm going to convince her that she belongs in my bed and in my life. That Milo and I are the best possible match for her.

> Then I'd like to take it. I can pay rent and watch Milo some of the time.

I blink at the time on my dash when I pull into my driveway. It's nearly four in the morning. Why is she awake? Maybe she couldn't sleep. She must have gone back to her sister's house and now the couch is bothering her.

> You don't need to pay anything. And watching Milo isn't required, either. My mom takes care of him most of the time I'm at work.

There's a long pause on the other side, so I unload my gear and take it into the garage before entering the house. It's quiet and dark.

> You have to let me give you something, or I'll feel guilty.

I can feel the anxiety radiating off the message. I suppose I understand that. She doesn't want charity.

> Okay. Then we can trade for babysitting. And if you feel inclined to cook...

> I'm happy to cook.

I enjoyed watching as Phoebe showed Milo how to crack an egg, and I think it'll be good for him in so many ways to have her around.

I wince. True.

She doesn't answer that, and I wonder if she's gone to bed, or simply doesn't know what to say. Finally, her reply comes.

Moving Phoebe in is easy when all she owns is a trash bag full of clothes and her computer equipment. I help her carry it down the block from her sister's house to mine.

"I need an office chair," is the one thing she says after we deposit her minimal belongings in the spare room. All I have are a desk and a bed, having never really needed the chair.

"There's an office supply store nearby," I say. "I can drive you."

"They have *so* many pens there!" Milo's blue eyes are bright and starry. "Every pen in the *world*."

Phoebe gives me an odd look, but I just shrug.

"He loves pens."

PHOEBE

It didn't take much persuading for Sandra to give her blessing for me to move in with Hank. She was all too eager to get rid of me, so I know it's for the best.

After depositing my things at Hank's house, the three of us head over to the office supply store. Milo browses the highlighters with shock and awe while I survey the selection of desk chairs. I pick something within my budget, and Hank helps me carry the box out to the car. Milo gets a set of markers, playing with them and his new notebook while I set up the chair in the spare room in front of the desk.

A desk. Just for me. After my month of living under Sandra's feet, this feels like the one thing that's *mine*.

"Thank you, Hank," I say as he gets the wheels of the chair attached. "Thank you so much."

He turns the chair over and rolls it back and forth to make sure the wheels are seated. "I just put together a chair, no big deal."

I chuckle and shake my head. "No, I mean, for the room. Having my own space again... you don't know how much it means to me."

He gives me one of his rare smiles. "I'm glad we could give you that." He straightens up and pushes the chair under the desk. "Feel free to use the closet, the dresser, anything you want. This is your home now, too."

It sends a sharp pang into my chest. *Home.*

My home is gone. But maybe... this could feel a little like a safe place. Like a home away from home.

I smile in return, because he's already made me feel so welcome here. "I appreciate that."

Hank nods, then shows himself out, leaving the door slightly ajar behind him.

First, I unpack my few clothes, which I've been slowly acquiring paycheck to paycheck. Even though I don't have a house anymore, the mortgage payments haven't magically stopped.

There are some hangers already in the closet, and it's not long before I have my few things neatly tucked away where they belong. I fill up the desk with some new office supplies, then I sit in my chair.

It's eerily quiet with Milo coloring somewhere and Hank doing his chores. It'll be far too easy to get comfortable here.

Around five, after a few extremely productive hours at my new desk, I head into the kitchen to find out if I can help with dinner. But Hank's already there, taking a container of marinating tofu out of the fridge. Meat probably isn't so easy to eat with big, wide teeth like his, so I'm not surprised when their meal is mostly vegetables and starches.

At his direction, I get the rice going, and then I stand nearby while Hank fries the tofu.

"Milo likes that kind of stuff?" I ask.

"Oh, yeah. Kid is a freak of nature. Kind of a health nut without realizing it." Hank throws some broccoli into the tofu fry for good measure. "I've never told him what foods are good and what foods are bad. He just picked what he liked—which means a lot of broccoli and tofu."

I lean on the counter, watching him. "You're a really good dad."

He's done such a wonderful job raising Milo so far, with love and care. He must have really wanted a child if he was willing to go through DreamTogether.

"I try. Every day." Hank stirs some soy sauce into the pan. "I feel like there's so much I could be doing better, but—"

"You're doing amazing."

Hank's ears tilt back shyly. "Thank you. I knew being a parent would be intense, but I didn't realize quite how much."

I remember when Milo came down with the flu, and I thought my heart might burst out of my chest every moment he was in pain.

"I can see why. He needs so much, and you're the only one that can provide it. It's a lot of pressure."

Hank shoots me a surprised look. "Yeah. You're right. I'm lucky I have Mom to help out, though."

"And me, too," I say, and his lips curl in a grin.

"Yeah. And you, too."

Soon, dinner is ready, and Milo comes thundering down the stairs with five new drawings in hand. He thrusts them in front of me and insists I tell him what I think. Hank says that show and tell will have to wait until after dinner, and Milo whines before learning the contents of the meal—and then he hurls himself into a chair and starts spooning it onto his plate.

I'm mesmerized by the messy way he eats, and how Hank tries to help him. Milo asks what I think of the food, and I make sure to gush, so Hank turns his head away and scratches behind his ear.

When we're all done, I clean up, and wave Hank away when he tries to help. It all feels... natural. Easy. Comforting and warm. I love how Hank's sweetness emerges when he's with Milo, how he towers over him while looking through his drawings and complimenting them.

Then I have to hustle away after dinner to make something for Sandra. When I sit down to stay with her while she eats, she waves me off.

"I know that you're having a nice night with Hank. Go on."

I give her a grateful smile, and wave as I head back out the door.

At bedtime, Milo insists I go upstairs to read to him, and I can't possibly turn him down. He picks out a book about a mouse and a strawberry, and I read it to him from cover to cover twice before he falls asleep.

"He really likes you," Hank says as we exit the room, leaving the door slightly open. "He forced himself to stay awake."

Tremulous hope swells in my heart. I want Milo to like me. I want all of his little smiles. I remember how he cuddled up against me as I turned the pages of the book, and how his eyes fluttered as he drifted off, and I wouldn't mind reading to him again and again.

"I like him, too," I say. "He's such a sweet kid. You did good."

Hank nods, but an expression I can't read crosses his face, and he doesn't say anything else.

We head to the living room, where Hank flicks on the television and sinks into the big armchair. Immediately, Darla climbs up into his lap, settling herself on one of his thick thighs. He brings up my favorite cooking show, playing the episode before last.

"You like *Cooking to the Top*, too?" I ask.

"Oh, yeah. This season has been great."

We talk about our favorite competitors as we watch and bet on who will win each challenge. I'm almost disappointed that Hank is on the chair and not the couch with me, because all I want is to be closer to him. Seeing him now, remembering how he felt when we were at DreamTogether, my whole body is alert and craving him in a deep, incurable way.

It's just the pregnancy hormones. I have to be careful of that. Last time, I got pretty emotional, and didn't always make the best choices.

I have to remember that eventually, when my house is finished, I'll move out of here—and I want it to be on good terms. That will be much more difficult if things get complicated between us.

When it gets late, I head off to my new bed with a soft mattress and big pillow, and sleep like the dead.

sixteen

HANK

I KEEP EXTRA QUIET THAT NIGHT WHEN I TAKE MY COCK IN hand, knowing that Phoebe's in the room down the hall. I close my eyes and my head drifts back, my horns resting against the wall as I think about everything that happened tonight, every smile she gave me, every time her breasts strained at her shirt or her jeans gave me a great view of her ass. How she sat on Milo's bed with him, her arm curled around him, and read him a book in such a quiet, tender voice.

She's so painfully perfect, I just have to think about her on the breeding bench in front of me, that incredible, glistening pussy on display, to get off. I cover my groan with one hand, biting into my palm with the force of my orgasm.

Then I wipe myself up with a tissue and toss it in the trash. My cock is still hard as I'm thinking about her, wanting desperately to be inside her.

I don't know how long I'm going to last.

Now, when I'm away at work and Milo's home from school, Mom and Phoebe trade off looking after him. My mother watches him during business hours so Phoebe can get her work done, and then Phoebe takes over. Phoebe asked for a list of all of Milo's favorite foods, then went shopping to come up with new recipes he might like.

But now she has to prepare *two* dinners, one for us and one for her sister. So sometimes she makes extra and carries it over to Sandra's house in the evenings.

"Sandra is scary," Milo tells me. "I like her... but she's scary."

Phoebe bites back a laugh. "It's because Milo has hooves," she confesses. "Sandra hates nothing more than shoes in the house because she's terrified of tracking in dirt. But Milo doesn't have shoes, so Sandra's knitting him some slippers."

Milo wrinkles his snout. "Slippers?!" He clutches his little hooves tight against him. "I'm not gonna wear slippers."

But all Phoebe has to do is look sad for a moment, and Milo changes his tune pretty quick.

"I guess I will," he mumbles.

When he comes back a few hours later, he's wearing tiny knitted slippers on his small hooves.

"I sorta like them," he says, flicking his tail.

The first week that Phoebe lives with us is when her morning sickness starts. It surprises her one day at dinnertime, and she suddenly rushes from the room, hand covering her mouth. When I hear her puking in the bathroom, Milo leaps off his chair.

"Is Phoebe okay?" he says, eyes huge. "She's sick!"

"I don't know. Stay here." I rub his head before racing off after her down the hall. She's in the half bath, crouched over the toilet, heaving her guts out.

"Damn," she mutters as she sits up, breathing heavily. "Must have food poisoning."

I raise a brow at her. "How far along are you?"

She thinks for a moment, and then it dawns on her. "Oh, that's what it is. But I didn't get sick with Milo. Or—"

Before she can finish, she bends over the toilet again and pukes some more. I rub her back, keeping her hair out of her face as she gasps and moans. Milo peeks into the room, but I wave him away.

Phoebe barely has the energy to make it up the stairs to her bed, and Milo frets as I take away her half-eaten plate of food and wash it.

"Does Phoebe need to go to the hospital?" he asks morosely.

I curse to myself. We're going to need to tell him the truth soon.

"No, Phoebe will be fine. She's just not feeling well."

Uncertainly, Milo nods and finishes his dinner, but he's quiet for the rest of the night. Before I head to bed, I check in on Phoebe, and stand in the doorway for a long moment watching her sleep, wishing I had the words to tell her what she means to me, that I had the courage to ask her to be mine.

Every day that passes, my hunger for Phoebe grows. Her sister is doing better lately and able to get around, so Phoebe decides we should all have a meal together—me and my mother and Sandra—so they can meet.

I'm nervous about everyone getting along, but as soon as we're all at the table, charismatic little Milo takes center stage and no one can resist him.

"Darla told me she likes Phoebe," he tells everyone, then shoves some pasta in his mouth. "And Darla only likes me and Dad, so that's a big deal!"

Phoebe mock-gasps. "She likes me?"

"Yes. But she said you should give her more treats."

Sandra laughs. "That sounds just like what a cat would say."

"She also says I should get two desserts instead of one," Milo goes on.

This time, it's my mother who chuckles. "Darla sure has a lot of demands."

Milo lists off everything Darla says he should have.

"Dang, he really got your eyes," Sandra says off-handedly to Phoebe.

I sit up straight. *Oh, no.*

"Whose eyes?" Milo asks, perplexed. "They're my eyes."

Sandra covers her mouth. "That's right. They're all yours, of course!"

Phoebe shoots her sister a disapproving glare, but Milo is curious now.

"What did you mean?" he presses.

I don't like the direction this is going, but there's nothing I can do to stop the train now.

Sandra looks helpless. "It's just... you have really pretty blue eyes, Milo! Just like Phoebe. Right? Cool coincidence."

Milo blinks. "Co-insa-what?" Then he runs off down the hallway to the bathroom. I follow him just as he calls out, "Dad, I can't see my eyes!"

Phoebe is shaking her head at Sandra as I leave the living room, and help Milo up onto the counter so he can look in the mirror. He stares at himself, then up at me.

"Wow," he says. "I do have blue eyes like Phoebe. But Dad, you have brown eyes."

Shit. This isn't how I wanted to tell him.

"I know," I say cautiously. "Your mother has blue eyes, though."

"My *mother*?" He simply laughs at me. "I don't have a mother."

I cringe. I've always told him that his only parent is me. He knows that some of the other kids at his school have two parents, but it's never come up how his life looks different.

"You do have a mother," I tell him. "All little calves have mothers."

I pick him up off the counter and carry him back to the kitchen, where Sandra is rubbing her face and apologizing. Milo is quiet when I would expect him to be bursting with questions. Phoebe glances at me with a concerned arch of her brow, but I just shrug.

Maybe we got away safely tonight. But how long until he finds out? We can't hide it from him. It feels wrong to lie to my own son. Phoebe and I need to have a conversation.

After Mom and Sandra leave for the night, I lead Milo up the stairs for bed. I sit down next to him and pick up the chapter book we were reading.

He sets his hand on the page when I start with the chapter number. "Dad, who is my mother?"

I should have known. I frantically look around for Phoebe, not sure what I should say, but she's nowhere to be found.

"It's complicated, Milo," I tell him. "Maybe when you're a little older..."

"Does it have to do with the baby factory?" he asks, bouncing. "Am *I* from the baby factory?"

"Yes!" The answer just bursts out of me. "Yes, you're from the baby factory, too."

Understanding dawns on him. "So I have a mom, but she's at the factory? Making other babies?"

I nod quickly. "That's right. She's making baby number two right now. The one that will move in to Phoebe's room."

Milo frowns. "But where will Phoebe go?"

"Back to her house." This is getting out of hand, and fast. I put my hand over his. "This is temporary, Milo. Phoebe's house burned down, like we talked about."

His eyes drift to the floor. "I know."

"So when it's done being built, she'll go home, and the baby will move in."

Though I doubt we'll be able to hide for long where the baby-making is happening when Phoebe starts showing.

Milo nods in understanding, then picks up the book again and asks me to read it. Soon, he's asleep, and I tuck him into bed and turn off the light before stepping out with the book clasped in my hand.

Phoebe's at the table working when I come back downstairs. I let out a huge breath as I sink into the chair across from her.

"Milo now believes he's from the baby factory," I tell her.

"Thanks to Sandra's comment?"

I can't even feel angry. "It was bound to happen."

"We're going to have to tell him," she says with a frown. At least we're thinking the same thing, even though I know the idea makes her deeply uncomfortable.

"Are you ready for that?"

Her shoulders crumple. "No, not really. I'm not... I'm not someone's *mom*, you know? I don't know that I ever can be."

I think I understand. She didn't sign up for DreamTo-gether to be a mother herself, and she clearly hasn't realized how much she is one without even trying.

"Then we won't tell him right now." I nod down at her belly. "But... we'll have to."

Phoebe sighs wearily. "I know. Live to fight another day, though, right?"

I nod, then to change the subject to something more comfortable, I point at her tablet. "What are you working on?"

Phoebe looks vulnerable at this question.

"It's all right," I say, backing off. "You don't have to show me."

She shakes her head. "It's okay. I just... I lost all my art in the fire. This is the first piece I've tried to do for myself since then, and I already feel rusty." After hesitating, she turns the tablet to face me. It's a canvas covered in foliage, each edge neat and crisp. I'm amazed at how many individual plants there are in the rainforest she's created. It has depth and dimension.

"Oh, there's a monkey," I say, pointing to a little brown head hiding behind a leaf. "And is that part of a tiger?"

"Yeah." She turns the tablet back toward herself and continues drawing even while she's speaking. "I'm making it for Milo, so he can pick out all the animals."

I bite my lip. She's making it hard to stay in my own chair. I'm overwhelmed by how much there is to Phoebe, how many layers she has waiting to be peeled apart and discovered. My heart wants to know all of her, just like my body does.

Fuck. I flare my nostrils and set my teeth. I can't keep holding this all in. I have to try.

"Phoebe," I start, and her head jerks up. I realize I've

been silent for the last five minutes, and she's gone back to drawing. "Sorry. I just... I mean, I want to say..." I've never been great at words, but this is especially bad.

"What is it, Hank?" she says, her blue eyes gazing up at me. Instantly, my cock starts to slide out of its sheath under my jeans.

"I, um..." I take a few deep breaths. "Phoebe, I really like you. I like you a lot. And I think you like me, too."

Her mouth falls open.

"Hank..." she begins, her face falling, but I don't want her to finish—not with that tone of voice.

"Please, just give it a chance between us," I barrel on. "We don't have to tell anyone. Milo doesn't have to know. My mom doesn't have to know. We can keep it quiet, and then if it doesn't work out, it's—"

"Okay."

I'm not sure I heard her right, so I flick my ears forward and cock my head. "Okay?"

"Okay. Let's try it." Phoebe puts down her stylus.

That's not what I expected her to say, so I sit there like an idiot for a good five seconds before I finally catch up.

"Really?" I don't know why I'm asking, because I shouldn't look a gift horse in the mouth.

Phoebe snickers, then gets out of her chair. "How many times do I need to say it? But you have to promise me something."

I hold out my hand to her. This is my opportunity and I'm not going to fuck it up. "Anything."

"Promise me it won't get weird. That if something happens between us... I don't want this to change. I can't afford a place of my own, not until the house is done."

I think my mouth falls fully open. "I would never make you move out, Phoebe."

But she doesn't relent. "Please, promise me."

I take two steps toward her, then sweep up her hand in mine. "I promise. No matter what happens between us, you can stay here as long as you want. You'll always have a place in this home."

Her face relaxes, and a shy smile takes over. She squeezes my fingers in return and closes the gap between us.

"Then show me this *something more*," she says.

seventeen

PHOEBE

I'M DOING SOMETHING SUPREMELY STUPID, BUT I JUST CAN'T help myself. Not with the meek way Hank asked me. It was impossible to say "no" to that face, his ears pressed back, his big, brown eyes looking anywhere but at me because he was so embarrassed.

His hand is warm and big enough that mine vanishes into his palm when he closes his fingers. Hank glances down at the place we're linked, and one of his rare smiles tugs at the corners of his muzzle.

"You're so beautiful, Phoebe," he says, so low and quiet I have to strain to hear him. "I've been thinking it since the moment I saw you."

I try to remember when that was.

"At DreamTogether?"

He laughs. "No. When I found you in your bathroom. When I saw your face for the first time. I thought you were the most gorgeous woman I'd ever laid eyes on."

"Huh?" I'm mystified. "But I was covered in ash, and my hair was all messed up, and I was *naked*—"

He uses my hand to pull me toward him, stopping my voice in my throat. He circles me with his arm, and here, I can smell him, and that musky, masculine, animal scent... I breathe Hank in, bringing up a hand to stroke the soft fur sticking out of his shirt.

"I know," he murmurs into my hair. "And you were still gorgeous."

Hank rubs his nose against me, then encircles me with both arms. Now our hips are flush against one another, and there's a prominent bulge in his pants rubbing against my belly.

He doesn't say anything else, and I think the time for talking is over. I lean back and tilt my head up so I can get a good look at him, and he runs a hand softly down my back. His nose lowers to mine, so I can feel his hot breath against my face. But he's afraid of being too bold, I can tell, so I push myself up onto my toes and press my lips to his muzzle.

I'm met with a sharp inhalation of breath, then Hank fists his hand in my shirt to pull me closer. His much bigger lips crash into mine, and it takes a moment for us to figure out how our mouths fit together. But once we do, the sheer *wanting* in that kiss almost overwhelms me.

Hank's lips are deft and sensual, timid but warm with need. As he cups my ass with his other hand, I sag against him—so he lifts me up off the floor with one arm hooked under me.

Now his mouth is dominating me as he nibbles my lower lip, then runs his tongue along it as if tasting me like a fresh fruit. I don't need to wonder how much hunger he's had saved up for me because it's all coming out now in the way he's holding me up in the air, devouring me and insisting I open for him.

So I do, and then our tongues meet in the middle. They writhe together between us until he pushes his tongue in deeper, and suddenly I'm very aware of the fact that we have, indeed, fucked before. That Hank has put his cock in me the same way his tongue is currently conquering my mouth, and holy hell, did it feel incredible.

A buzzing sensation begins at the base of my neck and it's quickly working its way downward. With his hands already holding me up off the floor by my ass, I lift my thighs to wrap my legs around his hips. Hank grunts as my jeans rub over his, right on top of his erection.

"I'm taking you up to my room," he says in a rumbling voice, like an animal's growl. I nod in agreement, and he keeps me wrapped around his hips as he practically jogs up the stairs. At the top, he carries me down the hall to his room, where he uses his free hand—I can't believe this guy can carry me with *one hand*—to open the door.

It's pitch black in here thanks to the heavy curtains, but Hank has no problem bringing me to the bed in the dark. He leans forward, cradling my back as he slides me down onto it. Then he stands up again and turns on the bedside lamp.

"You're pretty handsome, too," I say, struck by how utterly sexy he looks bathed in the faint yellow glow of the light, from his curled horns to his bulky chest, which strains the fabric of his shirt, down to his flicking tail.

Hank surveys me on the bed, and reaches out without speaking to brush his hand over my collarbone. The palm is bare skin, but he's furry beyond that, and I want to touch it— but I also want to see what he's going to do first.

He traces my sternum down between my breasts, over my shirt to my belly button.

"I'm glad we can look at each other this time," he murmurs, splaying his hand over my stomach. "So this is where our calf is growing."

Our calf. Our baby. Just that one word sends a shiver all the way down my body, electrifying me. We already made Milo, who's the most wonderful little boy to exist. Who is growing inside me? What will they become?

I think of how he put it there, how Hank stuffed me full of his cum over and over, and I sense myself getting wetter. All he would have to do is touch me and—

His hand travels southward, from my stomach to the mound at the crux of my legs. His eyes never leave mine as he winds one finger between my thighs, and applies firm pressure to my clit through my jeans.

I squirm under him, my hips rolling into his hand. He slides that finger down, then up again, glancing over my sex.

"You're good at that," I manage, gasping at the friction.

"Ever since that first time," Hank says, still watching me as he rubs me harder, "I've dreamt about this pussy."

Whoa. I didn't expect such dirty talk from him, but there's a gleam in his eye as he languidly taunts me through the fabric of my jeans.

"You did?" I ask breathlessly.

"Every night. For months afterward." He leans down closer to me, his big nostrils flaring. "For *years*."

He thought about me for that long? Just like I thought about him?

Hank breaks our eye contact to fiddle with the button of my jeans, and once it's free, he peels them down my ass, bringing my underwear with them. My pants aren't even all the way off my legs before his hand is between my thighs again, his fingers trailing along just the edges of my swollen lower lips. He uses his hoof to kick the jeans the rest of the way off my ankles.

"You're already so wet," he whispers, one finger skating across my pussy, up to my clit, where he gently circles it.

I smirk. "Probably because there's a gorgeous minotaur teasing me."

With a chuckle, he takes my thighs roughly in his hands and pulls them apart, spreading me out on the bed.

"Finally." His wide tongue darts out and licks his lips as he plays with me, his other hand roving down his belly to where his cock is straining his pants. He rubs it through his jeans while playing me like a fiddle, rubbing my clit before sliding back down, where he doesn't even penetrate—no, he glances over my outer lips, giving me an appetizer of what he could do and nothing more.

Then, he pulls away and yanks off his shirt, tossing it aside. He's fucking glorious, every last inch of his furry hide and thick muscle. I'm distracted when Hank kneels in front of the bed and wedges his big head between my thighs. I squeak as he dives into me with his mouth, his tail going wild behind him.

He sucks my clit between his lips and laves over it with that wide tongue, which pulls a sudden cry from my lips. I cover my mouth quickly, thinking of Milo sleeping only on the other end of the hall, and Hank chuckles against me.

"He's a good sleeper," he says, then drags that incredible tongue up and down. His curled horns are right in front of me, so I grab onto them as he licks me again and again, urging me down a dark tunnel toward the bright light at the end. I hear a zipper, and picture Hank with his cock in his hand while he furiously licks me, and I'm dying to know what it looks like.

"Hank," I say, tugging on his horns, but I don't think he can feel it. "Hank. Get on the bed."

He lifts his head, and I crab-crawl away from him, beckoning him up here with me. Obediently he rises to his feet, kicking off his jeans, and that's when I see it: the massive cock hanging between his legs. It emerges from a fur sheath, and it's long and cylindrical, with a blunt, flat head.

I know what that feels like inside me, and it sends a shudder from my throat to my pussy. So I wrap a hand around his arm and pull him down onto the bed next to me.

"Phoebe?" Hank asks curiously, landing softly on the comforter. But I don't answer as I awkwardly flip my position until I'm lying alongside him head-to-toe, so that monstrous cock is right in my face. My mouth waters.

"There we go," I say, reaching out to wrap one hand around it. Hank gasps the moment I touch his flesh. I'm going to worship this cock.

He gets the message about what I want to do immediately, lifting one of my thighs into the air so he can dive between them. His tongue lances out and brushes over my clit, sending a tremble through my body. After a few experimental strokes of my hands around his thick cock, which earns me another grunt of pleasure, I bring him into my mouth.

I feel Hank suck in his breath, then he goes wild on my pussy, running that tongue over me while I sink him ever deeper between my lips. Soon we're moving in the same rhythm, tantalizing each other, sending our pleasure around in a circle that never stops. I can't believe this thing fits inside me, because I can barely take it in up to the middle before it's too deep in my throat.

That will take some practice.

Hank is devouring me with frenetic speed, and then, he plunges a finger into me. I'm glad I'm being choked by his cock because it muffles the sound that comes out when he begins to stroke, burying his finger deep and then going to town with his mouth.

I'm definitely going to come like this.

His cock is weeping on my tongue, drizzling warm, salty cum. I make sure to lick the slit along the broad head, and Hank's hips jerk under me. Curious, I venture even further and take his furry balls in my hands. I pop his cock out of my mouth as I massage them.

"These are how you did it, hm?" I ask, continuing my work on his balls with one hand while I stroke his length with the other. "That's how you put this baby inside me?"

He huffs against my pussy, pushing his finger in deeper and licking my clit even faster. I'm so close to exploding, and he knows it, so he speeds up his attack.

"That's right," he hums against me. "I put it all inside you, and now..." He slides a second finger in, widening me for him. I haven't been using the dilator—or anything, really—while I was sleeping on the couch. I'm more sensitive than ever, and probably not as flexible as I need to be. "It's going to be such a good, strong calf."

Stars fill my vision as I take him back between my lips and suckle the head of his cock. I need him to feel how I feel, how I want nothing but him. How I've *wanted* nothing but him for so, so long. Now he's curling both fingers inside me, stroking them against my inner lining while flicking my clit with his tongue, and I'm a fucking goner.

"Hank!" I cry out, but it's muffled by his cock in my mouth. I suck on him harder while I orgasm, trying with all my might not to touch him with my teeth as my body tremors and shudders. My climax pulses through me, pleasure ricocheting across my nervous system.

Fuck. I haven't come like that in ages.

"Phoebe." Hank withdraws his fingers, which are soaked with me, and his cock pops out of my mouth as he sits up. I reach for it again, but suddenly Hank is on top of me, pinning me down with his hands while his haunches settle around my hips, and his hooves hang off the bed. There's a wild look in his eyes. They're big and dark, his brows drawn tight together.

"When I come," he says in a low voice, "I'm going to come inside you."

Oh.

"I would love that," I whisper back.

Hank's hand drifts back between my legs, and there, he wiggles two fingers inside me. His breath comes hot and fast, his pupils blown so wide they take up his whole iris. His horns blot out the overhead light, body so big on top of mine that I feel like I might sink into the bed. I writhe as he suddenly pushes a third finger inside me, and my body doesn't know what to do with it.

"You're so tight," he grunts. "I need to get you ready for me."

My entire body lights up like a firecracker about to go off. He twists his fingers, spreading my wetness all around before his panting grows too urgent. Then, he pulls them out and rubs them all over his cock.

I didn't consider the odd angle of his hind legs when I imagined us on his bed together in missionary position, but Hank has no trouble curling an arm under my hips and lifting them into the air, his other hand gripping the root of his cock. It's dripping even more for me now, and I need all of it.

"Please," I whimper, reaching down to spread myself for him. "I've missed you."

Hank squares his big shoulders, eyes riveted between my legs, and guides us perfectly together again.

eighteen

HANK

PHOEBE IS UNDERNEATH ME, IN MY BEDROOM, ON MY BED. She's really here, spread out in front of me on her back, splayed like an offering. That beautiful pussy is open and waiting, its pink wings spread and pulsing. She's so small, how can I possibly fit there?

But I know that I can, because I've done it before. So I press the blunt head of my cock into that open slit, and watch myself slip into it. I groan, overwhelmed by just the sight of it.

And oh, fuck, how she *feels*. How my body detaches from my soul as those folds with the delicate, curly hairs widen for me, soft but resilient as I push through. She accepts me so readily, slick with the spill from her orgasm, and there's nothing on this plane that compares to being inside her again.

My eyes roll back in my head the farther I fall into her, and then I remember—almost too late—that I need to be careful, because she's human and small, and I am very... not.

I grip her ass, completely ensconcing it in my palm, and breathe heavily as I try to get my senses back.

"Hank," Phoebe whines, pushing her hips against me so I slide even farther in. My balls shiver at the sensation of her around me, at the sight of her underneath me. Her big eyes are closed in bliss. Her tits are perfect, just like she is, and they spread to either side of her sternum with their broad, pinkish areolas and tight nipples. I wonder what it would look like with our calf sucking on them, and I have to try it out for myself.

When I wrap my lips around one nipple, Phoebe arches into my touch, so I bring it into my mouth and tease it with the blunt tips of my teeth. She squirms and her pussy clenches around me, so I repeat it with the other, remaining halfway sunk inside her.

"Please!" She wriggles under me, begging me to fuck her, but I'm in no rush. I'm going to savor every last morsel of her.

"Shh," I tell Phoebe, pressing in a fraction deeper. "Just warm my cock for a while."

I move to her other breast, holding her captive with my hand under her hips, and bring the other one into my mouth. As I suck on it, Phoebe moans underneath me. I want to make her scream, but I also don't want to wake Milo.

Maybe I need to soundproof my room.

I luxuriate in the feeling of her spasming around me with every nip of my teeth. Then I move up her breast to her collarbone, where I lick off her sweat with my tongue. She tastes fucking marvelous.

I rock from side to side, remaining at the same depth but testing all of my angles. I know Phoebe's body, and the thing she wants most is for the head of my cock to rub against her upper wall, only halfway in. It's much easier at this angle, on top of her. I test it a few times, nearly pulling out and then thrusting in partway, and Phoebe's big, blue eyes fly wide open, her lips parting to reveal her white teeth and pink tongue.

"Hank!" she cries, trying pitifully to keep her voice quiet. "J-j-just like that!"

I grin, because I plan to wring many more cries from her that she'll have to hold in.

It's only when I put my lips on hers, sinking into her soft mouth, that I finally thrust purposefully, seeing how far she's opened for me. I'm surprised when I sink in almost up to the base of my cock, and Phoebe muffles her cry with my mouth. I kiss her harder, soaking up each of her moans as I pump my hips, drawing them back and then shoving myself in again, making sure to hit that one spot with every stroke. Her body begins to shake violently, and her hands grip my fur, her fingernails biting into my skin.

She is amazing, my Phoebe.

"Look at you," I murmur to her, fucking her at a steady but lavish speed. "You take me so well. You're perfect."

Her hands clutch me tighter. "How do you feel so good?" she asks between moans.

"Because I was made for you."

I continue in a regular rhythm, denying myself the release I'm already desperate for. No, I need to see Phoebe finally crack, to reveal the soft creature underneath who holds her heart so close.

I circle one arm around her head and nuzzle her cheek with my nose as I pinpoint that place over and over again. She's crying my name, trying to keep quiet but failing, her thighs now wrapped around my waist. I anchor her against me, clutching her hips tight as I chase each of her incoherent sounds, until I have to kiss her again to keep her from waking up Milo.

And then, she rewards me.

Phoebe comes like an earthquake, rattling me to my very bones. Every muscle in her body tenses and suddenly I can barely move my cock, squeezed this deep and tight. I've spent so long holding off on my climax that it's almost painful now, but still I pump in and out of her. There's a wet *slap!* with every thrust as she reaches her pinnacle, her release coating both of us.

"Hank!" Phoebe sobs into my mouth, and it's the sound of my name on her lips that finally sends me careening into the darkness. I let out a low moan as I ram myself into her, and my explosion bursts out of me. My animal brain is telling me to bury my cum deep, to put yet another calf in my future wife, so I hold my cock there as I spill and spill. There's so much of it that soon it's running down my balls, and Phoebe is panting wildly underneath me.

I bring her into my arms, and she winds her hands around my neck with a happy sigh.

There she is. The sweet, tender animal inside her. She clings to me like a leaf in the wind, her legs still trembling where they're wrapped around my waist. It's so marvelous to be with her again, to smell her scent, to feel her around me, to get to see her lovely face as I bring her pleasure.

My eyes feel tight, like my face is too small for them. It's the way I felt when I saw Milo for the first time, when he was just a sobbing infant, coated in a thin layer of white and brown fur and wailing with his eyes squashed closed. Then he had opened them, and when those unusual blue irises looked up at me...

"Hank?" Phoebe asks in a small voice. She slides her hand down my cheek, up to my eye, and catches my tear with her fingertip. Her bow-shaped lips purse, and her brows tilt down.

"I'm just—" I wince at the crack in my voice. "I'm so glad I could look at you, Phoebe."

Tears spring to her eyes, too, a moment before she buries her face in my neck.

"I'm so happy," she says, though I can only make out half of it with her voice muffled. "It was... amazing."

Slowly, I withdraw from her, because I want to hold her in my arms fully. My cum sloshes down her thigh onto the comforter, but I ignore it, curling one hand under her legs to bring her into my embrace. My hand brushes over her toes, and Phoebe shivers.

I pause, then return to her foot, sliding a hand down her ankle to her heel. She shivers again as I run my fingers over her toes, and she curls into me tighter.

"Sensitive?" I ask, tilting my head down to peer at her. She has such tiny feet compared to my big hooves, and they're so fragile. I imagine they're also sensitive when she has to wear shoes everywhere.

Phoebe nods as I run my fingers over her toes again. They're dainty, but when they flex, I'm amazed by them. Soon I'm massaging her flesh and she's making quiet, pleased sounds, snuggling even deeper into the fur of my chest. It won't be too long before I'm hard again with her rubbing against me like that.

When I take her a second time, I lean back and rub her little feet while I fuck her, and she has to bite her hand to keep from crying out my name.

PHOEBE

Damn, the man has moves.

Man, minotaur, whatever. But wow, the way his abs flex as he plunges that cock inside me, how his pecs go hard as bricks as he crouches over me, completely encircling me with his arms. His neck is so thick that I think it would take three of my hands to go all the way around it.

The way he speaks to me in that low voice, telling me how good I am, simply enjoying me? He's a monster, and he's mine. Right now, with my head resting on his big bicep, his gentle breaths ruffling my hair while my hands tangle in the fur at his chest, I think that for tonight, Hank can be mine.

Unfortunately, my watch buzzes at five in the morning so I can find my way back to my own bedroom before Milo wakes up. I don't want to deal with the questions that might come if he found us curled up together, totally naked, in Hank's bed.

Fuck, we're going to have to deal with that. But maybe, just for a little while, we can hold this spark between us in our hands so only we can see it. If we were to tell Milo, that would invite all sorts of questions that I'm not ready to answer.

For now, for this tiny moment, I want to enjoy what I have.

By this time, I know the name of Milo's teacher, and even some of his classmates. The goblin is used to seeing me, but whenever he says, "Milo, your nanny is here," he quirks an eyebrow like he knows it's not the whole truth.

Thank goodness the morning sickness passes quickly so I don't have to worry about Milo asking more questions. But suddenly, I want nothing to do with half the food in the fridge. Everything smells bad except for fried chicken, and I make Milo and Sandra both come with me to get Crunchy's frequently. We spread out a picnic blanket in Hank's yard to enjoy the fading warm weather, and Sandra makes sure that Milo uses plenty of napkins on his greasy hands.

Unfortunately, it hasn't been convenient yet for a repeat of the night Hank and I had together given our vastly different sleep schedules. But he promises that he's swapping with someone else soon and will get a different shift for the next few weeks.

One of the other side effects of being pregnant: I'm ridiculously horny. It wasn't like this last time, but somehow, being around Hank has cranked it up into overdrive. I definitely masturbated while he was at work last night, and I've been thinking about the sight of his bull cock ever since he made me come so hard I saw the afterlife.

And then, finally, we end up on the same schedule. As much as I love Imelda, dinner that night drags by. Then I run over to Sandra's, where I try to act like I'm not in a rush, even though Hank is putting Milo to bed right now and soon, we're going to be alone together. Again.

My sister has a funny look in her eye when I set out the meal I brought over.

"You seem... spritely," she says, her lip quirking. "Something good happen?"

I try to school my expression, even though half of my brain is stuck on the prospect of seeing Hank naked later.

"Just thinking about work. My boss really liked the art I turned in today."

Sandra totally doesn't believe me—I can tell by her face —but she just says "Hmm" and finishes eating.

Imelda's still there when I get back, even though Milo's gone to bed. Hank shoots me a look while his mother talks about her latest book club book, and that look says everything. The moment we're alone, he's going to carry me up those stairs again, drop me onto that bed, and fuck me. And maybe tonight, he'll fit all the way inside me.

That would be incredible.

Finally, after what feels like hours, Imelda gets tired and says goodnight. The second she's out the door, though, Hank is on top of me, hands gripping my shoulders and lips meeting mine. Soon his palms are kneading my breasts over my shirt, and his eyes roll back as he fingers my nipples through the fabric.

Then I'm up against the wall, and Hank has one knee between my legs, his thigh methodically rubbing there. I hold on to him and ride it, letting the friction of my jeans do the work against my clit.

"I can't wait," Hank whispers to me, sliding his hand into the band of my pants, down to my underwear. He dips his finger inside them and takes no time in finding what he's looking for, and sinks the pad of his finger into my pussy. I moan underneath him, and he covers my mouth with one hand.

"I know what I need to do," he says, continuing to rub me while I whimper into his palm. His brow arches, and his lip curls. "I'm going to cover up that mouth of yours so Milo can't hear you scream."

A bolt of lightning blasts through me at the suggestion, and I nod furiously. Whatever it is Hank's dreaming up, I want it. I'll go anywhere he's willing to take me.

nineteen

HANK

I HAVE JUST THE THING: A STRIP OF RIBBON I USED TO MEASURE myself when I was ordering a suit online for a coworker's wedding. I was his second-best man, though I'd never heard of such a person before.

The ribbon is black and shiny and wide, perfect for wrapping around Phoebe's face. I ball up a bunch more around the middle, where it'll fit inside her mouth, and add to my mental grocery list to try out a ball gag.

The few dates I've had aren't usually serious, because my schedule is too hectic and, frankly, most women don't want what I want. But I've watched enough porn to get a good idea.

I've watched a *lot* of porn. Usually thinking about exactly what I get to do now.

Phoebe's on my bed naked, waiting for me, every last pale inch of her calling my name. I sit down on the edge and tell her, "Turn around."

Obediently, she pivots so her back is facing me, and her

breaths are coming fast as I reach around her face. I wad the ribbon in her mouth, then wrap it twice around her head before tying it off. She looks so pretty this way, and maybe I'll get even more ribbon. It would look nice around her hands, too.

The idea of Phoebe's tiny wrists bound behind her back, her ankles together and her pussy in the air... I'm so hard that it hurts to be inside my jeans.

She watches me as I remove them, a smile in her eyes as they fall off my hooves. It's a relief that she finds me attractive after so much time being anonymous. Of her own accord, she spreads her legs, revealing that fine, curly brown hair and the pink slit underneath it. My shirt goes next, and then my underwear, before I crawl onto the bed. I take one of her hands in mine, then the other, so both of her little wrists are in my fingers. Then I raise them over her head and pin her to the headboard.

"Are you ready now?" I ask. She nods rapidly, and her hips rise toward mine. I'm fully swollen for her, throbbing with my need to be inside her.

I crouch down, straddling Phoebe's hips, with my cock splayed across her belly. Her eyes are big and round as I rub the head over her skin, marking her with my pre-cum. I should lick her first and prepare her for me, but with that pretty gag in her mouth, all I want to do is make her scream into it. Still, I tease her plenty first, dragging the head of my cock down across her tiny clit, over and over, dipping it inside her as if I'm going to fuck her and then moving away again. Soon she's whimpering and rolling her hips, encouraging me to finally sink in.

So I do. The wonder of watching my cock slip between the spread leaves of her pussy fills me with glee, but I keep my movements careful and slow as I push farther inside her.

I thrust experimentally to see how ready she is for me, because I'm going to bury myself up to the hilt in her tonight. She moans against the gag, her voice coming out a muffled *mmph*.

I push some of her hair away from her eyes, staying shallow. "Look at how warm you are. So wet for me." Phoebe's head falls back as I hold her hostage at this depth. "The mother of my calf."

Her thighs spread even wider, her legs wrapping around my hips as she tries to bring me in deeper, but I resist, still pinning her hands down.

"And you'll look so good," I grunt into her ear. "So good all full up with me. I can't wait to watch my calf grow in your belly."

Those sapphire eyes find mine, and they get bigger as I target that place she loves. I can tell talking to her is turning her on by the way her pussy clenches and squeezes around me.

She mumbles an answer, but she's interrupted by her own growing moans.

Still holding her wrists hostage with one of my big hands, I lift her ass with the other so I can raise myself into a crouching position, and then I *really* fuck her. I let out a low groan as I sink in, using her body like a doll's. Phoebe releases a cry into the gag, and she clamps down on it with her teeth. I shove her even harder against the headboard, reeling my hips back and slamming my cock into her again, squeezing even more of myself through.

"Look at you," I murmur into her ear, holding her down even more fiercely as her body bucks underneath me. "So beautiful. Absolutely perfect. Everything I've ever dreamed of."

"*Hnnk*," Phoebe sobs. She's so wet that I slide easily in

and out of her in a steady, punishing rhythm, until she's trembling all over and her hips are snapping up into mine with every thrust.

If she weren't already pregnant with my calf, I'd be putting another one in her tonight. She's so lovely, so beautiful under me, her pussy swallowing me like it was created to do it.

This is our secret, for now. But I will prove to her that the future I see for us is what she wants, too.

PHOEBE

This is nothing like the breeding bench.

At last, I do scream into the gag as Hank finally pushes in all the way, until my clit meets the thick fur at the base of his cock. It brushes me wonderfully with every stroke, and I dissolve into a shivering mess of begging.

Hank leans his head down closer to me as I chant "please, please" into the gag.

"What is it you want?" he asks with a voice that's low and painfully seductive. He slows the movement of his hips, and I moan in protest. "You want to come?"

I nod rapidly, trying another "please," but it's too muffled. Hank grins and kisses me once on the nose before sitting back. He finally releases my hands, and instead grabs me by the hips, pulling out his cock abruptly. He turns me over like I'm a toy to be positioned how he pleases, and yanks my ass up into the air. I barely have time to grab the blankets before he pushes into me again, and I let out a cry muffled by the gag.

I love that I don't have to be quiet as he takes me with renewed vigor. There's nothing in the world like being with Hank again, like being filled by him and hearing his guttural groans. This is what I've always wanted, what I've always craved. I've been waiting my whole life for it, and now I get to have it.

Hank. For this moment, in this room, I can have everything I want.

Before I know what's happening, my vision is exploding in white, and I'm screaming into the mass of ribbon. Behind me, Hank lows like a bull as he smashes through my orgasm, but he's swelling larger and larger inside me, and before my first climax is over, I'm rolling into another one and he's groaning as he unloads.

Hank nearly collapses on top of me, panting. His arms shake as he holds himself up behind me, while I'm flattened into the blankets, my ass still in the air. With supreme gentleness, he slides out, and his cum gushes down my legs. Then he rolls us both onto our sides and curls himself around me, reaching up to free me from the gag.

"That was incredible," I say, rubbing my cheeks where the ribbon bit into my skin.

"Mmm," is all Hank answers, and it fascinates me how much he talks when we're fucking, and how little he talks when we're not. He brings his haunches up underneath me so we're spooning, and buries his nose in my hair.

I set my alarm, then let myself drift off in Hank's arms again. It feels much too good, much too right, and I know I've already fallen for him.

Damn it.

Once again at five a.m., I stumble back down the hall to my own room. I wish I could simply stay all night with Hank, cuddled up against my beast of a minotaur, but I can't. Everything becomes much too complicated if we have to explain what we're doing to Milo, not to mention my sister and Imelda.

Luckily, Hank has the following day off. We start out the day meal planning, then make a long list of everything we're going to pick up at the store.

"I want to get things you like to eat, too," Hank explains when he invites me along to do errands. "So it's not just tofu and broccoli all the time."

I try to reason with him that I don't need a special exception, but he's firm on the proposal, so I give in. Imelda offers to stay home with Milo so we can get through our chores faster, to which the little minotaur boy objects, but then Grandma bribes him with baking brownies and he easily gives in.

Then we're off in Hank's car, leaving the suburbs behind. Before we stop at the store, though, Hank continues on down the highway.

"Where are we going?" I ask, watching the store fly past us.

"Oh, well, I figured we had a few hours where my mom and Milo are occupied, so..." He trails off without finishing, then takes a quick exit. I watch out the windows as the buildings thin out and the trees get taller, and soon, we're pulling into Mirror Park.

Hank reaches into the back seat and grabs a backpack. "I threw together some food," he says. "Thought we might have a little picnic, just the two of us."

"Sneaky, sneaky. I'm impressed."

Hank gives me a rare grin. "Thanks."

He finds a parking spot and then puts on the backpack, and we hike off into the trees along the gravel path. There's nobody else out on a weekday at noon except one or two people walking their dogs on the other side of Mirror Lake. After a few minutes, Hank seems to find the perfect spot, and he leads me off into the grass on one side of the path. There's a grove here, where some brambles hide us from anyone walking by, and that's where he settles and pats the ground.

"Sit with me?" he asks.

It's so peaceful out here with birds chirping up in the trees that when I sit down, the stress leaves me in a whoosh. I breathe in the fresh air and fall back into the grass, spreading my arms and legs.

Hank chuckles. "Good, huh?"

I nod, staring up at the perfect blue sky with the occasional puff of cloud. "Beautiful."

"Yeah, you are."

I turn one critical eye on him and he chuckles to himself, then opens the backpack to pull out whatever he's brought along. First, he takes out a familiar placemat from home and sets it down on the grass. Then he removes some food I recognize: bread and gouda cheese, which is one of the few cheeses I can bring myself to eat right now; dried figs, which have oddly become a favorite of mine since Imelda started bringing them over; and a whole pile of cashew nuts, which I've been craving terribly. I only mentioned it in passing the other day, but he remembered.

Hank arranges it all just-so on the mat, then leans back and spreads his arms wide for me. "Eat up."

"Wow." It all looks so delicious, when nothing has appealed to me in days. "Thank you."

I make a sandwich with the bread, but it's dry and so is my mouth.

"Any beverages?" I ask, pushing my luck.

"Oh, right!" Hank sits up straighter and rummages through the front pocket of the backpack. Then he withdraws a pair of...

Juice boxes.

"No!" I fall backward dramatically. "Not apple juice!"

"It's mango *and* apple juice," he corrects. "The best flavor."

"There are no good flavors of juice box!" I cackle and roll back over to look at him. "Water would have been fine."

"Sorry. I did forget that."

He's really a dad through and through. He even has the stupid jokes to go with it.

I watch him as he eats, carefully placing one of each type of food on his bread before stuffing it in his mouth. When he chews, his whole huge jaw moves.

He arches a brow when he catches me staring. "Do I have something on my face?"

I bite my tongue to keep from telling him, *No, you just look beautiful, too.*

But that feels like stepping over some sort of line. What we're doing right now, having this secret date at the park... that line is growing blurrier. When I agreed to "something more," I wasn't sure what that meant—I just knew I wanted it.

Now what does it mean?

I shake that thought away because I don't want to ruin this moment. I have plenty of time to ruminate when I have to scuttle back to my room in the middle of the night and inevitably can't fall back asleep.

"Yes," I say instead. "There's a crumb on your cheek." So I reach out and dust an invisible crumb off.

"Oh, thank you." His hand snakes out and finds mine, and he wraps his huge fingers around it. "And thanks for coming out with me today. It's nice to have some time with you that's just... us."

The more romantic he's getting, the more uncertain I am. This is what I feared when we started sleeping together—that it would, inevitably, become this.

Gently, I pull my hand away and sit up like I needed to do that all along, then make myself another sandwich. He follows it up with a little bag of my favorite candy, and I become as melted as the chocolate.

Damn it. I'm in love with this minotaur.

twenty

HANK

I HAVE A PLAN, AND I THINK IT'S WORKING. I COULDN'T outline exactly what the steps are, but my intention is clear: sway Phoebe into marrying me. I want to ditch DreamTogether. I know we could survive without it if we worked as a team. She already fits so perfectly into our lives. Seeing her belly get rounder, watching her read to Milo at night or playing with him in the bath—and getting herself all wet in the process—makes me long for it.

I saw how she pulled away when I touched her hand. She's afraid of real intimacy, of getting any deeper than the amazing sex we've already had. As if that hasn't been life-altering. I know she feels it, too.

But I will change her mind, whatever it takes, however many romantic dates. I know what I want, what I *need*, and it's Phoebe.

I kiss her head as we clean up lunch, and trot away with the backpack before she can say anything. After packing up the car, we hurry through the rest of our errands, so it's not quite as obvious we took a detour.

That night, I stand in the doorway while Phoebe reads to Milo, her voice softening the closer he gets to falling asleep. Eventually, she trails off mid-sentence, then sets the book aside and tucks him into bed.

When she steps out into the hall, I run a hand down her back, over her ass. She twitches, and I know I do to her what she does to me. With a gentle push, I start down the hallway and she follows, my arm still around her. I'm excited about what I have planned tonight.

Finally, I have Phoebe naked on my bed, and I reach into the closet for the soft rope we bought at the store today. Her eyes bug out of her head.

"Is *that* what that's for?" she asks, aghast. "I thought it was for the tree out front!"

I shake my head very seriously. "It's for you." I unwind some of the rope, then without me even asking, Phoebe puts her hands together and holds them out. She still looks shocked, but there's a glitter of excitement in her eyes.

I thought she'd like this. She enjoys when I push her down or toss her around.

First I wind the rope around her wrists, tying it like I saw in a video I watched. Then I tie it to the post on the headboard so she can't get away.

"If you need me to let you down," I instruct, "tap the bedpost."

Phoebe nods. "Got it."

Finally, I hold up the ribbon from the other night. "So you can scream."

"Please," is all she says in answer. So I ball up the ribbon and stuff it into her mouth again, tying it around her head.

Once she's gagged, I take off my own clothes, simply admiring her as I do it. Standing in front of the bed, right where she can see me, I wrap my hand around my cock and stroke. Then my other hand snakes out, between her legs, and she lets out a muffled sound as I pet her there. She's already wet for me. I prop one leg up on the bed as I pump my cock from root to tip. Her eyes are fixed on it, her hips lifting off the bed as I run my finger over her sex, up to her clit, circling and teasing.

Then, without warning, I drop down onto the bed and yank her legs apart. Phoebe squeaks as I descend on her with my mouth. I easily squeeze a finger inside her, then another, going right for her weak point. All I have to do is lick hard in short bursts, curling my fingers to rub her, and she's already on the edge.

"*Hnnk!*" she moans into the gag as I go faster, harder, unleashing one of her orgasms and then continuing despite her protestations as I lead her into another. She writhes against her bonds, and I'm so glad I tied her up.

Once her pussy is good and warm for me, the pink folds swollen and a droplet of her release dripping down, I sit back on my haunches and grab her around the hips, pulling her toward me. Gripping my cock, I carefully guide myself inside her.

Fuck, she's tight from coming, and it takes everything in my power not to simply ejaculate now.

I lean down and suck on her breasts while I fuck her languidly. When I stop and take my breath, luxuriating in her, Phoebe tries to object through the gag. She pushes her hips toward me to take me deeper, but I shake my head.

"Just milk my cock for a little while," I whisper to her, reaching down to pet her clit. Instantly, she tightens around me, and I grunt at the sensation. I continue that until she's almost on the edge of her climax, and then I slam my cock deep, burying it in her pussy all while I rub her.

She bursts immediately, and I can't help but answer her, that beautiful clenching of hers undoing me completely.

Afterward, when I've untied her and cleaned us both up, Phoebe has a blissed-out look on her face.

"It's... nice," she says as I climb into bed with her, sorting the sheet and blankets. "Being tied up. I never thought I'd like it, but with you, I do." She leans back so her head is resting in the crook of my neck. "I trust you."

That's the loveliest thing she could have said to me.

"Thank you," I tell her, kissing the top of her head and pulling her in closer. I don't say the rest of what I'm thinking —just how deeply I've fallen in love with her—but maybe someday soon, I won't be able to keep it bottled up anymore.

PHOEBE

"Phoebe?"

Milo's voice startles me out of my focus zone. We've been drawing together at the table for more than an hour now, but it went by in a flash.

"Uh, yeah? What's up?"

He cocks his head and sniffs the air. "I finally figured it out."

"You figured what out?" I assume he means his drawing.

"Well, you smelled strange today. It's because you smell like my dad."

Oh shit. He can *smell* that? I should've taken a shower

first thing this morning, but after that thorough fucking last night, I slept in too late when I got back to my own room.

I guess I'll have to do it from now on.

"I don't know why," I say innocently.

That's when Imelda walks into the room. "What don't you know?"

"Phoebe smells like Dad," Milo repeats, eyeballing me. Imelda's eyebrow quirks.

"Well, she does live here," the older minotaur says, kneeling next to her grandson. "You probably smell a lot like your dad, too."

"Yeah, but not like *that*," he says rather mysteriously.

"All right, go get cleaned up for dinner." Imelda starts tidying up his crayons and pens as Milo grumbles and climbs out of his chair. When he's gone, though, Imelda gives me a knowing look.

"Hm," is all she says, and it's all she *needs* to say, because we both know what it means.

Fuck. So much for keeping what I'm doing with Hank a secret. If her sense of smell is as precise as Milo's, she probably knows all about it—and probably has for a while.

I wish Hank would've warned me.

When we're finished preparing dinner, I pack up some of the food and head down the block to Sandra's house. With fall settling in, it's dark out, but the lights are all off inside save for the shine of the television screen.

I push the door open slowly so I don't surprise my sister. She glances up from the television and nods.

"Hey," I say quietly, closing the door behind me. I approach the table and set down the half-full casserole dish. "Brought some chicken mac 'n' cheese that Imelda and I made."

She sighs as I go to grab her a plate. "Leftovers again, huh?"

I wince. I know I haven't been around as much as before, what with Milo needing so much of my attention. This is what I feared when I got mixed up with Hank—that I would slack in my duties to my sister.

This is why having what I have with him is impossible.

"I'm sorry," I amend quickly. "I'll come over tomorrow after work, and we can—"

"Stop, Feebs." She pauses dishing out the food to hold up a hand to me. "You don't need to apologize for living your life. I'm glad you moved in with Hank, and I'm happy you have a relationship with Milo." Then, Sandra waggles her brows. "And whatever is going on with the baby daddy... I'm excited for you."

I stare at her. "What?"

"It's obvious. You're suddenly all smiles lately. It must be because you're getting laid."

I blanch. Shit, was I that obvious? We're really not good at this "hiding our relationship" thing if we've gotten found out twice in one day.

"Yeah, thought so," Sandra says, tasting her food.

"It's not like that, though. We're just..."

"What, just having sex? Again?" She lets out an irritated sigh. "You did this already. You know you like him. You *more* than like him. So just admit it already."

"I can't!"

The volume of my voice surprises both of us.

"Why not?" Sandra truly looks like she doesn't understand. "Everything has been lined up right in front of you, Phoebe. You love Hank. You love Milo. He's your son. You even get along with the mother-in-law. Isn't that the best you could ask for?"

"I'm not Milo's mother. You said it once, and you were right. I carried him, he has my DNA in him, but he's not my son. And I don't know if I could ever be that for him."

Saying it aloud hurts more than I expected.

"It wouldn't be fair of me," I go on, my voice cracking. "I would disappoint him. I wouldn't make a good mom. And... I'm going to leave."

"Why would you leave?" Sandra asks.

"When my house is finished!"

She gives a sad shake of her head. "I'm just going to ask the same question: why? Sell the house. Move in with Hank. Have a baby together. What's so wrong with all that?"

I hiss through my teeth. "I don't know how to be a parent, Sandra! I watch Hank do it, and I'm just in awe of him." I choke back tears, thinking of how much he loves Milo, how good he is at caring for him.

She doesn't get it. None of them get it.

"Do you know why I kept those letters?" I ask quietly.

My sister furrows her brow. "What's that matter? They're gone now."

"I kept them as a reminder. As a *lesson*. Not to be like them."

She looks even more confused now. "Is that what you're worried about? Our parents?"

"I don't have it in my blood, Sandra. To be a good mother to Milo, to this new baby. I come from bad stock."

She gasps. "Don't say that!" Her fork rings as she sets it down hard on her plate. "You are nothing like our parents, Phoebe."

"You don't know that."

"Then learn from Hank," she says. "Read all the parenting magazines. I don't know why you refuse to see the happiness standing right in front of you."

I swallow hard, avoiding her eyes. It's just too much to commit to them, to both of them and the baby inside me, in the way Hank wants.

"Don't hurt him." Sandra narrows her gaze at me. "Don't lead on Hank if you really intend to move out later."

I bite my lip. Now that I've had a taste of him, I couldn't possibly give up what we have.

But she might be right. If I don't plan on staying, I should cut it off now.

twenty-one

PHOEBE

THE SHORT TRIP BACK TO THE HOUSE FEELS LIKE WALKING TO the gallows. Can I really end things with Hank? The idea of it, of saying those words to his face and watching him fall apart... that might break me.

I rack my brains for the right answer as I step in the door, finding the kitchen lights off. Imelda is in the living room, reading a book in a chair. She must have put Milo to sleep while I was gone.

We make a good team.

I sigh as I walk into the living room, ready to be interrogated again now that she knows what's going on between Hank and me. But Imelda just looks up over the top of her glasses at me and arches an eyebrow.

"Sandra liked the mac," I tell her.

"Oh, good."

When I don't say anything else, neither does she, and she goes back to her reading. I guess I'm surprised, but also not that surprised Imelda doesn't want to talk about it. She seems to be a firm believer that her son's business is her son's business, so I head to the guest room to get ready for bed.

But I lie awake for an hour, and then two, puzzling over the right thing to do. My hand absently rubs over my belly, where I imagine Hank's baby growing. Wouldn't it be good, though, to be here when I need help later on in the pregnancy? And then... if I stayed, I wouldn't have to hand it away to someone, never to see it again.

It would ruin everything I have with DreamTogether. Would there be repercussions for us? I need that money to pay my mortgage and Sandra's.

It's too tangled, too complicated. Finally, after counting a thousand sheep, I manage to drift off.

I wake up to a muzzle in my face, lips pressing against my cheek.

"It's me," Hank says in a low voice, kissing down my neck. He scoots me over on the bed easily, then climbs in beside me.

I wonder what time it is. It must be early in the morning.

"You should be in your bed," I say, interrupting myself with a gasp when he nips my throat with his blunt teeth.

"I should be where you are." His hand slides down my arm, over my hip, where he grips me harder. "I should always be where you are. Especially when you're big and round with my calf." He cups my belly, which is now just starting to change shape.

"Hank..." Just his name sticks in my throat. "Milo noticed today. So did your mom."

He pulls back. "Noticed what?"

"Imelda knows now. About us. I think our moment of keeping this a secret is over."

Hank's ears flatten, and his brown eyes turn worried. "Did she say something to you?"

"No. But Sandra did."

He sighs. "I guess it was bound to happen."

"I think it was. And it made me realize... I shouldn't be doing this with you if I'm not serious about it."

There. I said it. It feels like a stone falling into my gut, but I did it.

Hank is silent for a long moment, his hand still curled under my belly. Then he pulls me closer and nuzzles my hair.

"Then marry me."

My brain comes to a stop. What?

"Say that again?" I ask in a whisper.

"Marry me, Phoebe." Hank sits forward, taking my hands in his. "Let's be serious, then. Let's tell Milo. Let's get married, and—"

"I can't, Hank." I sigh and pull my hands away. He lets them go, his hopeful expression falling. "You don't understand. I can't be a good mom to Milo. I don't know how to be. I don't think I can be what you want."

He furrows his brow. "You are what I want. Right now. You don't have to try or be anything different."

I don't say anything. He thinks I'm what he wants because of his hormones, because we're living together, because of the baby.

"Phoebe," Hank says in a serious voice. "I love you. I don't even need to think twice about it to say it. I love you so much, and I think we could be wonderful together if you gave me a chance."

My heart swells hearing it just as much as it breaks. I

want to crumple into his soft arms. I want to accept everything he's offering me, but can I really step up and be the person I'd have to be?

"You'll be an amazing mom." His smile lights up his whole face as he cups my cheek. "There isn't anyone better. Milo adores you, almost as much as Darla."

We both snicker at this.

"And he's a sweet kid, Hank," I say, rubbing his arm. "But... you don't understand. I didn't have good parents. Not like you. I had a terrible example, and I don't know if I can be what Milo and this kid"—my hand glances over my belly—"need."

Hank is quiet for a long time before he finally answers.

"You haven't told me about your parents. I actually know very little about you, Phoebe."

I'm surprised to hear him say this. He's never outright asked me, so I never thought to tell him. Maybe I'm a little protective of it, of Sandra's and my past.

I still feel like somehow I'm at fault. Sandra says our parents were just bad people, but I've always wondered what I did to deserve it. What I did that made them decide they didn't love me anymore.

"My parents left us at home alone a lot. One of the neighbors saw us playing in the apartment hallway by ourselves and called it in. So we got moved into foster care."

Hank is watching me, just listening with his ears perked forward.

"They never tried to get us back. We wrote to them, hoping to hear from them, but they returned our letters. They didn't want us."

I don't cry as I tell him this story. I think I've already shed all the tears I can, years and years ago. But still, I feel the stab that first time a letter came back, and I thought it must be a mistake until our foster dad explained what the stamp meant.

"I'm sorry," is all Hank says. He tugs me into a hug, tucking my head under his chin. "I'm so sorry, Phoebe. No child deserves that."

I shrug, saying nothing more. I don't know how to put together all the words I feel about how inadequate I am, how woefully unprepared I am for the type of life Hank envisions.

"I don't want to pressure you," he says, rubbing his hand down to my shoulder. "You don't have to say yes or no right now. But just... think about it."

After a breath, I nod. "I can do that."

I'm not ready yet to end this, but neither can I accept his offer. I need to sort myself out first.

I'm grateful when Hank doesn't leave. He lowers his nose to my ear, nuzzling the shell of it with his lips.

"Can I persuade you?" he asks in a rough voice.

"Yes."

He gently tugs me down to the bed in his arms, my back to his front so I can feel him getting hard under his jeans against my ass. He unbuttons my pants and pushes them down, his hand finding its way right to where it belongs.

Hank knows just how to touch me to rile me up and uses his powers with abandon. While he fingers me, he shoves down his jeans so they're stuck on his hooves. He spreads the lips of my pussy, splaying them wide to make his way inside me easier.

I moan as he glides home, now that my body is well-trained to take his. His hand slides up my body, over my bra to my mouth, which he covers with his palm as he sinks in deep.

My cry is muffled, and the sensation of his palm

clamped down on my face is so acutely erotic that I spasm around his cock. Hank grunts, panting as he remains seated inside me. He likes to hold me this way, completely speared on his cock, soaking in me before he starts to move again.

His hand mutes another cry as he pulls out and thrusts in again, all while he keeps my thigh held up. Now he's fucking me relentlessly, sinking all the way in before yanking back out. I'm so close that I'm shuddering all over, but he maintains his rhythm, even and practiced.

"Yes, Phoebe," he murmurs to me, lowering his head to rest his cheek against mine. "Let go for me. Drench me."

I sob into his palm as I finally let it sweep through me. I'm a bird in a whirlwind, swirling around as Hank grunts behind me, and his cock fills me even more. One more firm thrust and he's releasing everything he has to give.

We're both reluctant to say goodbye after we've cleaned up. Hank kisses me on the nose, then trails his fingers through my hair.

"Rapunzel," he says after a beat, tilting his head. "That's what I called you the first time around. When you had Milo."

I blink. "Huh? Why?"

"Your hair." He pats my head, stroking it. "It was so long back then. But I like it short, too. You have the most beautiful hair."

I don't know what to make of that compliment as Hank releases me and gets up to leave.

"We have to tell him soon," he says as he reaches the door. "I don't want to rush you, Phoebe, but I think for Milo, we should make up our minds."

I nod in understanding as he leaves, shutting it quietly behind him.

HANK

I was ravenous for Phoebe when I got home from work. I needed to have her, just like I have every moment of every day. Now, I'm hooked on her. Her smell is a drug, her pussy a salve on my soul, her moans and whimpers all the music I need.

But she's struggling, I know. She feels like she's responsible for everything, like the weight of the world rests on her shoulders. I wish I could show her that she doesn't have to carry it alone, and we could conquer life easily if we were together.

Phoebe is willful, stubborn, and so full of heart when it comes to those she loves—and I wouldn't have it any other way.

I hope I haven't pushed her too much, but I do wonder what would happen if Phoebe left. As much as I've been certain I can convince her, I'm afraid of her hesitation and what it would mean for me and for Milo. He's gotten attached to her, too, and it might break his heart if she left.

No. I won't give up. Not when a perfect life with Phoebe as my wife is so close, so within reach.

I sleep like the dead that morning and afternoon, and wake up to the smell of dinner. Sandra is at the kitchen table when I come down.

"Feebs wanted me to spend more time with her," Sandra says by way of explanation, giving a little eye roll.

"Love you," Phoebe calls back.

I quirk a brow at her as I sidle in wearing my gym shorts and no shirt, not thinking we'd have company.

That's when Milo zooms into the kitchen behind me, carrying Darla. "Dad! You're up!" She wriggles in his arms, and he lets her go free. "We're having tem-poo-poo-ra!"

Phoebe slaps her forehead. "Not tem-poo-poo-ra again." She scoops some battered veggies out of the frying pan and strains them before dumping them onto a tray. "Sorry, Milo wanted breakfast for dinner, but Sandra and I outvoted him."

"No, it's perfect," I say. "I love tem-poo-poo-ra."

Milo screeches in delight, and we exchange a high-five. Phoebe groans even louder.

I'm reluctant to leave for work that night after I've put Milo to bed. But duty calls, et cetera.

When Sandra is gone, I pull in Phoebe for a kiss. She stiffens at first, but easily falls into me as I hold her the way I do when I'm about to haul her off to bed. I ravage her mouth, then release her, wishing I could stay another half hour.

"Go," she says, swatting me on the butt. My tail flicks as I grab my shirt and head out the door.

That night, though, I'm glad I showed up to work. It's one thing after another. We're called to the scene when an old man has a heart attack, but he's dead before EMTs even arrive. Then an alarm goes off at a college dormitory, and we arrive to a parking lot full of sleepy students in pajamas while their common room leaks smoke out the window because someone left food in the oven.

We scuttle all over town that night, and by two in the

morning, I'm run ragged. I'm glad I have my coworkers, who are all troopers.

Then, toward the end of our shift, we get another call. There's been a fire in a restaurant that has an apartment above it. We all race to the truck and get in, heading off down the road with our siren howling. You can already see the smoke billowing into the sky.

When we get there five minutes later, the whole building is in flames, radiating heat. We're not sure where the entrance to the apartment is, but the restaurant owner points us to stairs that are certainly not to code.

Ron goes up first, and I'm close behind him. When we smash open the front door, the apartment is filled with smoke, and I grab my mask and slap it on my muzzle. It doesn't help, though, with this much particulate in the air.

This is a bad one, and it's taken over most of the apartment already.

"There's rooms in the back and upstairs," Ron says after surveying the layout.

I beat him to the punch. "I'll take upstairs."

I'm halfway up the steps, blinded by the smoke, when I hear a crash and a scream. Uh oh. I hope whoever it is isn't hurt or trapped. I've been in situations like that before, and they still haunt me.

I race down the hall to where a door has fallen in. Inside is a little orc girl, trembling all over on her bed. She's the same age as Milo.

I barge in through the door and snatch her up, and though she flails, I hold her close to me.

"It's all right," I say through the mask. "Hold on to me as tight as you can."

She obeys, clinging like a monkey. I turn around to leave

the way I came, flames licking at us, smoke filling my lungs. Everything around us is blazing, searing my exposed fur.

Then the beam over the doorway cracks and falls, showering us with sparks. I cover the girl with my arms, but the sparks burn holes through my heavy-duty clothes, anyway.

With the door blocked, the only way out now is through the window—from the third story. I turn around, breathing in even more smoke as I consider my options.

No. I know what I have to do, so I hold the girl close.

"I'm sorry," I say to her. "I'm getting you out of here. Hang on."

Then I run toward the window and jump through the glass, which explodes around me. The shattered edges tear into my body as I go through. But I need to keep my charge safe, so I intentionally fall wrong, bracing myself underneath her to keep her from getting injured.

I hit the ground and hear bones snap.

twenty-two

PHOEBE

THE CALL WAKES ME UP FROM A DEAD SLEEP. IT'S A LOCAL number, and it made its way through my spam filter, so it must be something important.

I pick it up. "H-hello...?"

"Is this Phoebe?" asks a deep voice on the other end.

"Yes, this is she."

"Ron here. Hank's coworker. Hank's on his way to the hospital right now. You should go meet him there."

Wait, what? My mind reels. Hank, at the hospital?

"What happened?" I demand, sitting up straight in bed. "Is he okay?"

"No. He's not. Go to the hospital now, Phoebe."

Then the phone goes dead.

I leap out of bed, throw on my clothes, and rush up the stairs. I wake Milo by shaking him.

"Milo, we have to go. Come on."

Eventually I rouse him, and when he asks what's

happened, all I can say is, "Your dad. I don't know, but we're going to the hospital."

That's all it takes. Milo starts crying as we get in the car, frantic to know what might be wrong.

"I'm sure he'll be all right," I say, but it's an empty platitude. I have no idea what awaits us there, but my heart is beating a million miles a minute, my hands shaking on the wheel of the car.

I hope he's okay. I can't stand the idea that something happened to him tonight.

Finally, we're there, and I'm holding back my own tears as we find parking. When we get in the front doors of the hospital, we head right to reception.

"Hank Pittsfield?" I ask.

The receptionist eyes us.

"This is his son," I say, gesturing at Milo. "I'm the... nanny."

She clicks a few times on her computer, and I'm itching to demand she show us to Hank *now*. I need to know what's happened to him. Milo is still sniffling at my side, and I clutch his hand tighter.

"What's your name?"

"Phoebe. Phoebe Harrigan."

She clicks a few more times, and I'm impatiently waiting, grinding my teeth the more minutes tick by.

"ID please?"

I quickly slip it out of my wallet and hand it over, and she studies it before handing it back.

"Hank has you listed here. He's in the ER right now."

That's what I was afraid of.

I hold Milo's hand as we follow the signs toward the ER, turning this way and that but getting nowhere. Eventually, we're stopped by a doctor on the third floor.

"You seem lost," he says.

"I'm looking for Hank Pittsfield." Instinctively, I pull Milo against me and stroke his hair. "He's the firefighter."

The doctor's expression falters. "Oh, him." He nods for me to follow down the hall. "He's in surgery right now for his leg, but..." He shakes his head. "You should know he's inhaled a lot of smoke."

That's not what I want to hear.

He shows us to some seats in the waiting room. Milo cries in my lap, and I hold him tight, trying not to cry myself. I call Imelda to tell her where we are and what's happened to Hank.

Finally, we're allowed in to see him. My minotaur. He's hooked up to machines, all of them beeping. His eyes are closed, and his leg is splinted and wrapped. He's not moving.

Fuck. Not Hank. Please, not Hank. My face feels tight and my pulse thunders even faster, because I can't believe it's him there, beat up and unconscious.

"His heart is trying its hardest," the doctor says with a pitying look. "It's fighting, but it's an uphill fight."

Milo breaks into renewed tears and rushes to his dad's side. He grabs Hank's big hand with his tiny one.

"Dad!" he cries out, but his dad doesn't answer.

I kneel beside Milo and pull him into my arms, patting his newly trimmed hair. I have nothing to tell him to make it better.

"Is he going to survive?" I ask the doctor in a quiet voice.

He looks down at Milo, then at me, and lets out a resigned sigh. When he speaks, he speaks so only I can hear. "It depends on Hank. The next few hours are going to be critical."

At that moment, Imelda rushes into the room. She grabs Milo and hugs him tight as they both cry next to Hank's bed.

The doctor takes that moment to pull me aside. "I want to prepare you for the worst. If he inhaled too much, it could cause organ failure. Or he could have a heart attack."

My own tears finally break free as he says these words to me.

"We don't know," the doctor says quickly. "Hopefully he'll wake up soon—that would be a good sign."

Hank can't. He just can't. I still had so many things I needed to tell him. I should have said yes when he asked me to marry him, so he would know that I loved him even if we never saw each other again.

No, I can't think like that. I need to believe that someone as strong and determined as Hank can do it.

The doctor leaves us, and we all take up positions around the room as Hank's machines beep. Milo falls asleep with his head on his grandmother's lap.

"Tell me how bad it is," Imelda whispers to me.

I clench my hands into fists and breathe hard so I don't cry again. "They're monitoring his oxygen levels, which are dangerously low, and pumping him full of it."

She drops her head, and I rub her shoulder with one hand.

"I'm sorry," I whisper. "I'm so sorry."

"It's not your fault, Phoebe." She puts her hand on top of mine and smiles at me. "I'm glad you're here. I'm glad Milo has you right now."

I cover my face, the guilt nearly devouring me.

"He asked me to marry him," I finally say, hiding behind my fingers. "He asked me, and I said I didn't know. He told me he loved me, and I didn't say it back. What if... what if I never get the chance?"

I try to keep my voice quiet as it shakes.

"Oh, honey." She squeezes my hand. "You will. I promise

you will. Hank is a fighter. He's fought for you since the moment he met you, and he's not going to stop now."

What? Since he met me?

"At DreamTogether?" I ask.

"Mm-hmm. I think he figured it out the first time, when you had Milo. I'm almost positive he knew then you were meant to be."

Even back then, I was special to him? Just like he was to me?

Hank. The sturdiest man—or monster—I've ever met. As dependable as a mountain and yet so warm and vulnerable. He opened his home and his heart to me easily, and has never held it against me that I wasn't ready.

I can't let him go. Not ever.

As the hours pass, Imelda falls asleep, too. Soon, morning sun creeps in the high windows of the hospital room. I'm not sure how many hours have gone by when I hear Hank's quiet voice muffled by the oxygen mask.

"Phoebe?"

I sit up straight, and my eyes dart to Hank's face. His lids are half-open, like he's exhausted. His hand reaches for me.

"Hank!" I try not to say it too loud as I stumble over to the hospital bed. I wrap his fingers up in mine. "I'm so glad to see you!"

"You, too," he says with a faint smile. "I'm glad you were here when I opened my eyes." His gaze veers over to Milo, and his smile widens. "My sweet boy."

I nod and hold his hand tighter, wishing I could hug him. Milo and Imelda are still fast asleep as we whisper.

"Don't wake them up yet." Hank pulls me closer to him, and I kneel beside the bed. "I just want a moment to tell you how much I love you."

"I love you, too." I say the words without thinking twice. I kiss the top of the mask. "You'd better live through this, because I want to get to tell you that in front of everyone."

He pauses. "Really?"

"Really."

Hank chokes out a laugh. "If only I'd known all it took was almost dying."

My lips screw up. "You're not out of the woods yet."

"I know." He coughs, and the sound wakes up his mother and Milo. I step aside as Milo lunges for the bed.

"Dad! You're awake!"

Hank grins and rubs one of Milo's nubby horns. "I am. Good to see you, bud."

I watch the three of them together, hoping that this isn't the last time.

HANK

I drift in and out of consciousness. My chest aches, my throat is raw, and my nose feels like it's full of dust. Thanks to the drugs, I can't feel my leg. They say it will heal, but it'll be six months at minimum before I'm back on my feet again.

Which means no work, and puts even more stress on Phoebe and my mother.

But I'm glad I'm alive, and I'll hold onto that as long as I can. The doctors say I'm getting just enough oxygen to survive, but it's taxing my body. They're doing everything they can to keep me from having heart failure.

While I'm awake, I hold Phoebe's hand every moment possible. Milo adds his own hand to the pile, like we're doing a squad break, and Phoebe giggles as she brings him into her lap.

"You want to hold hands with us?"

He scratches his head. "Yeah. I like it when you hold hands." He leans back to rest his head on Phoebe's chest. "Do you guys like each other?"

Phoebe inhales sharply, but I have to smile.

"We do. At least, I like Phoebe."

Her face is already turning pink. "And I like your dad. A lot."

Milo's face is radiant at these words. "Wow. Cool. Darla will be happy when I tell her."

My mother and Phoebe take turns returning home and helping out Sandra. Sandra even makes the trip to the hospital to say hello and bring me some "adult-sized" slippers she knitted. I know it's so that I can visit her house.

It feels as if we've built a little family of our own.

I ask about the girl from the apartment above the restaurant, and I'm told she inhaled a lot of smoke, too. But she's doing better than I am and should be released soon. She was barely bruised in the incident, and her family sends me flowers and a balloon with a note that makes me tear up.

Soon, I'm spending more time awake than I am asleep. My breathing grows less shallow and strained, and they have to pump me full of oxygen less and less often. Hope blooms in Phoebe's blue eyes, and it helps to know I'm fighting for a life with her.

When the doctor comes back the following day, Phoebe asleep in the chair, he wears a slight smile.

"I think you're in the clear, Mr. Pittsfield," he says, looking over his chart. "There will be some long-term damage, but over time it'll improve as your body heals."

I'm buoyant. Utterly over the moon.

All it takes is whispering Phoebe's name and she wakes up. The doctor leaves us alone together as I give her the news, and she cries happy tears on my chest.

I'm free to go home under the condition that I return for routine checkups and testing. It looks like I made it through the worst of it, though the leg is still just as broken.

I'm given a cast and crutches, which are a nightmare to wield. Phoebe and my mother help me out to the car, and I'm sure this will just be the first of many times. It'll be months before the bone weaves itself back together and I can walk properly again, and there will always be a crack through my left hoof.

Then, at last, I'm home again. Unfortunately, going up and down the stairs is too much work, so I take up residence on a cot downstairs.

At night when the light is off, Phoebe sneaks down the steps, and I welcome her onto the cot with me. We can still make love as long as she's on top, so she's frequently in my lap, bringing my cock inside her at her own speed and angle. It's harder than ever not to go off early, with no control like this, but I get good at biting my lip and holding it back.

It's the worst time to be laid up. Everything takes five times as long with my busted leg, and while Phoebe's belly rounds, I can barely help out around the house. Usually the best I can do is entertain Milo, which he loves. It's wonderful to get so much time at home with my kid, but I also ache to be helpful, to be useful.

Luckily, I have the most fantastic family in the meantime. Sandra comes over whenever she can get out of bed for dinner, and sometimes we all pile into her small house instead. As the good weather fades, we take as much time as we can to barbecue in the front yard.

"I can't get over this book I just read," Sandra says from her camp chair. It's the special kind with a built-in footstool. "Just blew my mind."

My mother turns away from the grill top. "Oh, are you a bookworm?"

Sandra glows. "Yeah. It was kind of my hideaway when we were kids. I would just bury myself in a book when I felt sad or lonely."

They fall into a steady conversation about books while Milo drives his Big Wheel up and down the sidewalk. Phoebe stands next to me, and I don't think she even realizes she's had a hand cupping her stomach.

I hop over on my crutches and take over turning the hot dogs now that Mom has gotten caught up in a conversation and forgotten about them.

Everything feels perfect, but there's still one thing we need to do. We put it off after my fall, but now Phoebe's starting to show. We have to come clean with Milo.

After dinner one night, we all sit down in the living room while Milo arranges miniature horse fences around where Darla is sleeping on the floor. I clear my throat to get my little bull calf's attention.

"Hey, Milo. Remember a while ago when I told you that you have a mother?"

Milo cocks his head. "Yeah. I know who it is, though."

We all stare at him.

"Wait, what?" I adjust my leg in its cast so I can sit forward on the couch. "You do?"

"It's Phoebe, right?" Milo continues placing the fences until the circle is closed around the sleeping cat.

Phoebe and I gape at each other. Silence fills the room until my mother says, "Yes, it's Phoebe."

Milo shrugs as he plants a plastic horse figurine inside the corral with Darla. "Thought so." He finally sits back and glances up at Phoebe. "Do you work for the baby factory? Are you bringing the other baby here, too?"

Phoebe covers her mouth, and I can't tell if she's horrified, laughing, or both. Eventually, though, her shoulders sag forward and she says, "Yep. That's me. Except I don't work for the baby factory, Milo." She pats her belly. "I *am* the baby factory."

His eyes get huge and wide. "What?!"

"Yep. Your dad's new baby is growing right here."

I flinch at the way she says it, but I know that for now, it's true. The only reason I haven't bought her a ring yet is that money's tight while I'm out on disability—and I want to wait to give it to her until I can properly kneel.

"Wow." Milo gets up and walks over to her. "It's in there?"

"You want to touch?" she asks.

Milo's little mouth falls open, exposing all his blunt teeth. "Really?"

"Sure." She takes his hand and presses his palm to her belly.

Milo is aghast. "The new baby is in there?"

"Yep. It'll be a long time before it's a proper baby, though. Right now, it's just a bunch of cells figuring things out."

I laugh at this description. I love her more and more every day.

"Is this how you guys made me, too?" Milo asks, glancing

over his shoulder at me while his hand remains on Phoebe's stomach.

"Yup. Phoebe grew you there, too, just like she's doing now."

"Wow. Cool."

When Milo's curiosity is satisfied, he goes back to playing with his horses, and the rest of us let out a collective sigh of relief.

That went much, much better than I could have hoped. Now there's just the matter of getting better, and then I can seal the deal.

twenty-three

HANK

THE ONE UPSIDE TO MY INJURY, THOUGH, IS I GET TO SPEND plenty of time with Phoebe while she grows my calf. And that is the greatest gift I could have asked for.

We're still hiding that we're in a relationship from DreamTogether. It'll be more complicated to explain when I'm there in the room with her when she gives birth, but by then, it'll be too late. Maybe they'll withhold her final payment, but I think once I explain the situation, I can get us through it.

Phoebe goes in alone for her routine checkups, and though I wish I could be there, this is easier until our time with DreamTogether is up. The new calf is moving more, and Milo loves to hop on the couch and feel when it kicks.

"Did I kick like that?" Milo asks, astounded.

"You sure did. With your teeny little hooves." Phoebe plays with his feet, and he giggles and rolls around on the couch.

Phoebe plans to sell her house as soon as it's finished

being rebuilt, and that should produce a decent nest egg for the future. But I'm still stuck in my damned cast as her belly swells and her breasts get bigger. I want to do things for her, pick things up for her, lie on top of her while I make love to her, but I can't. It's a humbling experience, and I learn a lot about the different weights the women in my life have to lift to keep the household going.

Phoebe is doing more art these days, usually sitting on the couch beside me with her tablet in her lap. She makes pictures for Milo that are fun and playful, and even considers putting together a children's book. But then at night, she does... other kinds of art.

There are lots of ways to build intimacy, and I've learned so many of them outside of sex since I've been off my feet. Phoebe has me sit naked on the couch so she can draw me, and my cock gets thicker and harder the longer she stares and draws. Once she just drew a close-up of my dick, and then I held her in my lap and asked her to masturbate while looking at it.

One thing I can do is get some pussy on my face, so she frequently rides my mouth while I lie on the cot. She loves when I push my tongue inside her and fuck her with it, before returning to assailing her clit.

We watch movies together late at night, and play *Monster Masher* with Milo. I watch them cook meals together, weighing in when I can. Sandra, who also can't always stand up to help, plays cards with me at the table.

Sometimes Phoebe and I simply lie together at night on my cot, spooning while we talk. I stroke her belly, imagining our calf coming into the world, waiting for the right moment to take the plunge.

PHOEBE

As my belly gets bigger, Milo takes measurements of it, writing them down in scribble nonsense in a notebook. He gets a doctor's set for his sixth birthday because he's become so fascinated with the process of growing a baby, and he loves to listen to my belly while we're watching television.

I can tell that Hank is growing more and more restless by the day, but he's good at keeping it to himself.

We still haven't talked about marriage again, not since the hospital. I think Hank can tell that I'm working my way toward it, finding my footing here with him and with Milo.

He's not so subtle when he hands me the phone number for a therapist. He's been seeing one since his accident to help him work through some of the feelings of helplessness he's had.

"I've been thinking about what you said about your parents. I thought maybe you could go there and explore those feelings safely with some help."

I raise my eyes to his big brown ones, and I just want to fall into them.

So I do what Hank suggests and call the number on the scrap of paper. It takes us a few sessions to get into my childhood baggage, but once we're there and digging into it, I want to curl up and hide.

I'm glad that I have Hank after those sessions, when I'm tired and empty of tears and don't want to talk about anything anymore. He simply holds me around the shoulders and turns on a mindless TV show, his cast up on the coffee table.

One of these nights, after Milo's gone to bed, Hank brings me up onto his good thigh and simply rubs me between my legs, over my jeans. After a time, he pushes down his gym shorts enough that his cock pops out.

"Warm me a little, won't you?" he purrs, unbuttoning my pants.

I shuck them off, then, with my shirt still on, I sink down onto him, taking that thick cock as deep as I can. After a few moments, my body opens to accept all of him, and Hank settles his hands on my waist to watch the show over my shoulder. Every so often he reaches around and thumbs over my clit, and groans as I pulse around him.

"Look at you, such a good place for my cock to rest," Hank says, slightly canting his hips back and then pushing in deeper. He stops again, exhaling a long breath as he rests his chin on my shoulder.

We watch the show that way, his finger moving languidly on my clit, building me up to an orgasm and then letting me fall back down. He nips my neck, fingers my nipples through my shirt, and sometimes just watches with his arms around me.

Finally, I can't take it anymore, and I lift myself up onto my thighs. It's a lot of weight with my big belly, but I'm desperate. Hank chuckles as I drop down on him, taking everything I can inside me, before doing it again. He thrums my clit faster, whipping me up into a storm until I'm biting into my hand to muffle my cries.

When he takes me there, to our special home together in the stars, I know what I need to do. I've talked it over at length with my new therapist, about how much I *want* to be the person Hank and Milo need.

But I think that maybe Hank was right, and I might be okay the way I am.

We sit there, panting, until Hank's leg suddenly starts itching. He groans in annoyance. I separate us, then reach for the side table to get his scratcher.

"My fur under the cast will never grow back the same again," he grouses as he puts the scratcher in his cast.

"Hank."

He pauses and glances up at me, clearly surprised by the seriousness of my tone. "Phoebe?"

"Your cast comes off next week, right?"

He nods uncertainly. "Yep. Should be right as rain."

"Then..." I clear my throat. I've been thinking for so long about this, and now that it's here and I'm about to say it, I suddenly fumble the pass. "Then, um... do you want to, uh... get married?"

I can't look at him as I ask this question, because it's been so long now since we discussed it. But then a hand takes me by the chin, and Hank turns me back to look at him.

"Yes. Yes, I definitely want that." He leans sideways to kiss me, quick but tender pecks, half a dozen of them. "When? I'm game for anytime after this cast comes off."

"That's what I was thinking. Right after you're free."

His eyes widen. "A shotgun wedding?"

I take his hand and run it over my bump, which is nearly close to bursting now. "Seems appropriate."

He snorts a bit like a horse, and I love when he does that.

"Let's do it. We don't need anyone but Mom and Sandra, anyway."

I sit up on my knees, starting to feel excited. "Exactly. Let's just have a ceremony in the yard, and then a nice dinner out."

Hank gawks at me. "In the yard?"

"Good luck getting a venue on a few weeks' notice."

"Fair point." He leans forward and brushes his pink nose over my cheek. "Whatever you want. It's yours."

HANK

I'm absolutely over the fucking moon.

First, I get this horrendous cast off. I know my muscles are atrophied, and it's going to take time and physical therapy to get everything working right again, but freedom is so close that I can taste it.

And then... finally. I get to marry her. I get to have the love of my life forever, to raise our calves together, and all the joys that brings with it.

We break the news to the family the next day, and Sandra and Mom both understand the rush. Milo doesn't quite get the significance of "getting married," but he's enthusiastic about it because I am.

He's a little grumpier when he finds out he needs to get fitted for a tux.

We hurry the preparations, renting a trellis and buying fake flowers, and then it's finally time for my damned cast to come off. They can't get the saw through it fast enough, and I'm gritting my teeth by the time they get the bottom off my ankle.

At last. I'm free.

I put a slight amount of weight on it, and it holds, but everything aches. Oh, do I have a lot of work to do.

Immediately I'm hooked up with a few months of PT. I still can't return to work, not until the doctor gives the say-so, but I'm not upset about it. It means I get to be home when my calf is born, and I can't think of a better time.

Phoebe looks full and big in her wedding dress, and my love for her swells even greater as she walks out the front door, into the yard. Sandra went and got herself some kind of officiant certification, so she sits on a chair with me under the trellis as Phoebe approaches us.

I've never seen a woman so beautiful. Her bright eyes sparkle in the sun, and I could just fall into them. I sweep her into my arms, bracing all my weight on my good leg, and kiss her before Sandra can even read her piece.

My sister-in-law-to-be huffs. "Hank!"

Finally, I release Phoebe, and Sandra starts reading. She put together a wonderful story of how we met that's far less lascivious for Milo's little ears. He claps when he hears his part of it, how Phoebe couldn't resist him, and Phoebe blushes.

"And I'm so glad to welcome you in as my brother-in-law," Sandra finishes, tears in her eyes. "Thank you for taking such good care of her. I've never seen two people better suited for each other. I know you'll be happy for a long time." She sniffles. "Please kiss the bride."

So I do. I kiss Phoebe with everything I have, for all the years ahead of us.

And then, there's the wedding night.

Oh, fuck, have I been waiting a long time for this. I'm straining at my pants all throughout dinner just thinking about what I'll do to Phoebe later. She helps Milo cut up his food and chides him when he throws something on the floor. She's a little stricter than I am, but I think that's a good thing. He'll get balance in his life.

At last, we're off to the hotel room Mom got us as a wedding gift. It's fancier than any place I've ever been, but I barely have time to register our surroundings before I have Phoebe down on the bed on her back, bracketing her head with my arms.

"Oh yeah?" she asks, wiggling with her excitement. I love how horny Phoebe is for me now that she's comfortable with me—happy with me.

I grunt at the feel of her belly underneath me, full of our calf. We still have not had the sex revealed, because we find it doesn't matter to us. We're excited no matter what we get, and we'll come up with a name on the fly.

I relish her, kissing her until she's gasping and her lips are red. The whole time I rub her between her legs, over her underwear, getting her good and riled up.

It's our wedding night, though. I'm not going to move too fast. I'm going to savor my wife.

I shiver all over as the word ripples through me.

"Wife," I say aloud, touching my big nostrils to her tiny human nose. "My wife."

"That's me," she murmurs back, rubbing my ears. My tail sticks out straight and my balls contract, and I am quite ready to consummate this marriage.

twenty-four

PHOEBE

Everything starts off sexy on our wedding night. Hank's on top of me, his face buried between my legs, licking and sucking and sliding his fingers inside me, stroking and teasing until I'm a whining mess. And I don't have to keep my noises down. He doesn't have to gag me.

I can scream until I'm hoarse in a hotel room.

"I've wanted to do this for months," Hank says, groaning as he palms his dick. He's crouched on the bed with his tail flicking in the air behind him, hooves splayed. He returns to his work on my clit, ransacking it for my pleasure.

"Please," I moan, grabbing his ears, his horns. "Fuck me!"

"But you haven't come yet—"

"I know!" I'm so horny I can barely take it. "Put your cock in me, please."

He grins as he rises to his haunches. Hank's unsteady at first, still working on that new leg strength, but finds his place with his hips wedged between my thighs. He drags his cock up and down, and I groan with irritation.

"You want it that bad, huh?" Hank leans down as that blunt head navigates inside me. "All right then. *Wife.*"

I moan as he pushes in, his velvety cock slipping through easily to where it belongs. Hank's eyes practically roll back in his head.

"I like when you're on top," he says, withdrawing just enough that he can thrust back in. "But I missed this."

I circle my arms around his neck. "I did, too."

Hank lifts one of my thighs as he maintains a slow pace, his incredibly ripped abdomen flexing with every jerk of his hips. Sometimes I forget just how beautiful he is, how lucky I am to have him. And he's mine now.

"Phoebe." His hands encircle my belly as he fucks me in his own glorious, perfect rhythm. "I'm ready to have a family with you. To love you forever."

I'm surprised when tears come to my eyes. I've never cried during sex before.

"I can't wait," I answer, and Hank leans down to kiss me.

That is, of course, when my first contraction hits.

Damn it. I didn't get off, and now we're speeding to the hospital. I called DreamTogether with my phone, explaining that I was in labor. Now Hank is driving me there, with Imelda and Milo coming later, and I hope we don't totally fumble the ball.

We broke anonymity. What is DreamTogether going to do?

I'm led to a room and seen by the same doctor I've been visiting every few weeks, and he gives us an odd look as we sit down together.

"Boyfriend?" the doctor asks, eyeing Hank.

"The father," I say. Then I hold out my hand, which now has a single small diamond in a gold setting. "And husband."

"Hm." The doctor stares at each of us in turn, then shakes his head. "I swear, this place."

I don't know what that means, but I'm quickly distracted by another contraction.

It goes on like that for hours, the pain growing intermittently worse as time wears on. Eventually, Milo shows up, and I'm relieved to see him. I need his happy, wild energy right now.

He sits on the hospital bed with me and shows me his latest artwork of Darla as an angel. I don't know why he started drawing this, because Darla is fine and not anywhere near death, but he loves giving her wings and a halo.

Then the contractions get worse and more frequent, and much to his displeasure, Milo is led out of the room. Hank sits beside me and takes my hand, a mask stretched across his big muzzle.

"Ready?" he asks.

"Of course not. I never am."

He strokes my hair. "It'll be over soon."

I know he's wrong, but he'll learn.

HANK

Watching Phoebe go through labor and give birth to our second son is definitely the worst experience I've had, and I'm not even the one doing the hard work.

Bringing a new life into the world? Check. Watching your wife scream and moan in pain? No thanks.

I feel like Phoebe spends more time assuring me that she's fine than I spend comforting her. She just asks to hold my hand while she pushes, and her eyes screw up tight as she lets out a scream.

And then, after what feels like eons of pain, our wailing infant enters the world.

He's smaller than I remember Milo being, with many more brown splotches than white, more like my mother. The nurse brings him to us, and Phoebe is gasping as the woman teaches her how to latch.

"I've never done this part before," Phoebe says in wonder as our calf's lips wrap around her nipple. The crying abruptly stops, and soon he settles into her arms, his eyes still closed.

I wonder if they'll be blue or brown.

We whisper in quiet voices about names, eventually settling on Archie.

"Archie and Milo," Phoebe says, petting some of Archie's soft fur. "They could be their own team."

"Maybe in tennis."

I get up to bring in Milo and my mother, and Milo has clearly been told to behave himself because he moves slowly and talks quietly as he slips into the room.

"Hi, Mom," he says, walking up to the hospital bed. He simply started calling her this about a month ago, and Phoebe only smiled when he did it. "Wow. The baby's so small."

"That's right." Her voice is sleepy but pleased. "He's just little for now. But he'll get big like you."

"Cool." Milo pets Archie's tiny hoof. "Get big soon, okay? So we can play."

I'm grateful to have them home again the next day, and now that I'm on my feet again, I can finally help out. But poor Phoebe. This birth wasn't quite as easy as her last one. As tiny as Archie looks, he wasn't tiny coming out, and she has hell to pay for it.

I think we'll stop at two of them. I can't watch her go through that again.

DreamTogether was not pleased that we had connected —and gotten married—while under contract. Deciding we both broke the agreement, they barred Phoebe from working for them again. Not that she planned to.

They still gave her the final payment, though, so I can't be that mad about it.

Unlike Milo when he was a baby, Archie is a crier, keeping us up late at night. All it takes, though, is hearing his squeal of laughter as his brother makes a peek-a-boo face, and I remember why I did this. Sometimes I stand in the doorway to the nursery, simply watching while Phoebe holds Archie in her arms, nursing him. Her eyes rise to mine and she smiles a whole, big, pure smile, like she has everything she ever wanted.

Milo is obsessed with his brother, so excited for him to grow up. He attempts to feed Archie, but after getting covered in sweet potato goo, he decides it isn't for him.

It's wonderful having Sandra around, who likes to simply hold the baby in her lap while the rest of us busy about. Archie always calms down with her, like she cast a magic spell. She's knitted him plenty of adorable little outfits. And I'm grateful every day for my mother, who slides in to take over with the kids when we need a break.

Unfortunately, I do have to go back to work after a few months of being home with my wife and kids. But I'm looking forward to it, to helping people and trying to save lives again.

Even though my schedule allows me to be up at night to take care of Archie, by the time he's eight months old, we've both been run ragged. He's finally nearing the end of the worst of it—hopefully, knock on wood—and the nights are getting better.

"Hello, Hank?"

Mom startles me out of a daze. I'm at the kitchen counter with a giant half-eaten carrot in one hand, simply staring at the wall.

"Wow," she says, studying me. "Guess this couldn't come soon enough."

I blink away sleep. "What couldn't?"

She holds out a packet. "Two tickets to the Bahamas. For you and Phoebe, from me and Sandra."

I stare at her, then take the packet.

"What about Milo? And Archie?" I ask, hoarse with my budding excitement.

"We're going to watch them for a few days. You two need to get away."

I've never felt so relieved in my life. A few days away from the baby with just my wife? Fucking pinch me.

"Don't worry," Mom says before I get a chance to respond. "I cleared it with your boss before we got them."

I hug her as tight as I can.

"Thank you, Mom. Thank you so much."

I don't need any more incentive than that to run to the office where Phoebe is working and surprise her with their gift.

"One week from now?" she asks, hesitating. "Maybe you got time off of work, but I'll still have to call in."

"You've been working your ass off since the fire, and you barely took any time off when Archie was born. They'll survive without you for a week."

She sighs and nods. "Yeah, you're right. I'll let my boss know today. I have the vacation time saved up."

I let her go so she can make her call, feeling lighter than I have in quite some time.

PHOEBE

My house is almost done being rebuilt, so when I get back from our trip, it'll be time to put it on the market. I'm strangely excited. Ever since the fire, that house has held nothing but bad memories for me, and I'm ready to move on.

The money will be a big bonus, too, and we can tuck it away in a retirement nest egg.

My heart tugs as we pack for our trip, thinking about being away from Archie and Milo. Every day I feel more and more like Milo's mother. He snuggles up to me on the couch whenever we watch his favorite show, and hugs my legs when I come home. I love him more than I thought I could ever love another person. I understand now why Hank worked so hard to have him—his little laughs, and even his tears, fill my chest to bursting. I just want to make all the hurt in the world go away, and make sure he has the best life possible.

And watching Archie go from crying infant to wiggly

toddler has been a joy. I adore how his eyes close when he breastfeeds, and his little hands curl into fists. His tiny hooves are the cutest in the world, and even when he cries in the middle of the night, holding him brings me back to earth and soothes my soul.

But I know it'll be good for us to get away, and I certainly could use the time alone with Hank. Our sex life has not been what it used to be since Archie was born, and I miss it.

The plane ride is long, and I sleep against Hank's big shoulder most of the way. Then we're surrounded by sun and sand, and the pure relief washes over me.

I still worry about the boys while we're gone, but I know they're in good hands, and I'm able to let it drift out of my mind.

Hank and I make love every single night, and I can finally be as loud as I want. One night, after Hank has had a lot of rum, he picks me up before stumbling into the room. I giggle as he pushes me up against a wall, his cock already tenting his swim shorts. He's shirtless from the pool, and I get to admire him once again as he leans back, keeping me aloft with his hands under my ass.

"Damn," he says, his eyes catching on my cleavage inside my bikini. "My wife's really hot."

I wink. "So is my husband."

He kisses me then, all of his love and all of his lust in that press of his lips on mine. His hands fumble with the strings holding my swimsuit in place, but he does eventually free my tits from their bondage. Then his mouth is on them, sucking my nipples between his lips and groaning as I leak milk onto his tongue.

Yeah, that's definitely one of Hank's kinks.

He huffs with how horny he is, licking his lips as he swallows it all up. His eyes now half lidded, he makes his way down to my bikini bottoms and unties those, too. In response, I push down his swim shorts, and that delicious cock springs out.

"I need to be inside you," Hank growls. He becomes so desperate when he drinks that it's adorable. "Please."

I nod and lift my hips, rubbing myself against him. Hank grits his teeth as he feels around for where he belongs, and I giggle as I reach down to lead him to his treasure.

Hank moans as he sinks in almost fully in one stroke. "Fuck," he grunts, his neck bowing. "You feel incredible. Like nothing else. I'm addicted to you."

I wrap my arms around his neck so I can kiss his snout as he pulls out, nearly withdrawing, and then dives back in.

"So do you. Your cock is magic."

Hank snorts in that way I love, and his thrusts grow more frantic. He emits a long low as I get closer and closer to my climax, tightening around him with every feverish pump of his hips. Somehow, he holds me up with just one arm while he reaches down between us to flick my clit.

Oops, I'm a goner.

I cry out as I spasm all around him, and Hank roars like an animal as he fucks me faster. I grip the hair on the back of his neck as my orgasm wrings me like a wet rag, but Hank isn't done yet. When I've recovered, he throws me onto the bed.

"Get on your knees," he instructs, standing at the edge, his cock proud and dripping as it waits for me.

I do as I'm told, remembering the first time we met and he fucked me just like this. I'm still panting from my previous orgasm as he glides in, riding a wave of my wetness.

We go at it like that for what feels like hours, simply

enjoying each other, not worrying about anything back home. Once we're both sated, Hank collapses on top of me, his cum gushing out all over the hotel bed.

Good thing I went on the pill. With Archie being as much work as he is, I don't know if I can handle another one.

"I love you so goddamn much, Phoebe," Hank murmurs in my ear, rolling over so he can bundle me up in his arms. "Sometimes it's like my heart is going to explode."

I giggle against his collarbone. "I know the feeling. I always wondered what it would be like to love someone like this... and it's so much more than I thought it could be."

Hank smiles against my hair. Soon, I hear him snoring, which he only does when he's been drinking. I fall asleep in his arms like that, wondering how I got so lucky.

Our time away is wonderful, but after only four days, I'm longing to go home and see our boys. When we call, Milo gets on the phone, chatting our ears off about school and all the fun activities he's doing with Grandma and Sandra. We say goodnight to him every evening, and I wish I could hold him in my arms.

Finally, the plane lands, and we find Imelda, Sandra, and the boys all waiting outside security. Milo runs toward us, nearly bowling me over when he leaps on me. He's gotten even bigger, and I expect I'll only be more surprised each day by his growth. Hank picks him up and swings him around, and Milo lets out a delighted squeal.

And the moment I hold Archie in my arms again? I can't help the tears from flowing down my cheeks when I look into his perfect little face, and I kiss his forehead over and over. Sandra puts her arm around me, patting my shoulder, while Hank and Imelda exchange hugs.

That's when I know that I'm right back where I belong.

THANK YOU SO MUCH FOR READING!

I hope you enjoyed Hank and Phoebe's story! If you did, please consider leaving a review. Reviews help indie authors like me to find new readers.

Lyonne Riley published her first book at age five, which was written on tiny sheets of notebook paper, and she insisted on giving a copy to everyone she knew. She's been writing ever since, from fan fiction in her teen years to original fiction as an adult. After a stint in traditional publishing, she discovered what she truly wanted to write: very smutty stories about monsters and the little humans they worship.

Now she lives in the middle of nowhere with her dogs and spouse, writing sexy fairy tales.

acknowledgments

I would like to thank everyone involved in helping me through the process of putting out this book. I can't say enough how much I appreciate the help and encouragement of the people around me—especially Amber, who told me I could do this in the first place.

Huge thank you to Rowan Woodcock for the gorgeous cover illustration. To my critique partners, who gave me phenomenal feedback: You all make this possible. And of course, my amazing spouse, who has always supported my dreams—and given me lots of inspiration for my characters' sexy adventures.

I couldn't have done this without the expertise of my fellow self-published romance authors. Thank you for inviting me into your circles and helping me through this process.

And thank you to my readers, who gave this book a shot.